About the Author

This is the author's debut publication.

The author has a master's degree in business administration from MONIRBA, University of Allahabad, as well as a doctorate degree from the University of Canterbury. He is a fellow of the Royal College of Teachers, England. He is also a Member of The Royal Society of Literature, England.

The author hails from an illustrious family of doctors (ophthalmic surgeons) and, in his own words, 'decided to deviate into management to give the patients some rest!' Being a direct descendant of Diwan Rai Gurbuksh Singh, diwan to the erstwhile Maharaja Chet Singh of Benares, the author revels in all that is imperial, ceremonial, martial, and simply ludicrous!

Having done his schooling from Boys' High School & College, Allahabad, the author gives full credit to the school for shaping him into an acceptable human being with frequent canings and adherence to the school motto, '*Mentem hominis spectato non frontem*'.

An all-India university boxer, accomplished bathroom singer, and intrepid yodeller, he prefers to entertain his bathroom fittings with early morning caterwauling. Having business interests in real estate, education, and food, he lives in Allahabad with his mother; wife, Smita; and children, Devesh and Riticka. As also their smelly mastiff, Samrat!

Praises for the Book
A Ship of Many Oars

'Short and crisp. Doctor Srivastava's deft use of language as well as vivid descriptions for the readers keeps them longing for more!' (Suhail Mathur, bestselling author of *The Bhairav Putras*).

'The author expresses himself subtly yet expressively, allowing the reader to soak in the tale. Covering a wide array of genres, this book should be certainly read' (Himani Gupta, noted book reviewer and critic).

'Simple, uncomplicated plots. And then, like a wind, the end hits you. Hard. The signs of a potentially gifted storyteller exist in Niraj's writing, so much so that you wish the stories were longer' (Saurabh Chawla, author, blogger, and core team member at *Storizen*, India's most popular literary magazine).

'Interesting! A commendable collection of riveting short stories that can find a place in the best of anthologies. The book leaves one yearning for more' (Sanjeev Mathur, editorial head, *The Book Bakers*)

'Good concepts, tastefully done. The writing is engaging, and having written short stories myself, I could appreciate the hard work put in by the author, which has come out effortlessly' (Durgesh Shastri, author of *Curse of the Red Soil* and founder of Inkcraft LLP).

A Ship of Many Oars reveals the master storyteller in the debutant Niraj-ji. There is an old-world charm in the narrative and the choice of words and expressions. These nine crisply written stories will linger in the minds long after the book has been read and placed in its home on the shelf' (Pawan Kumar Mishra, international Vedic astrologer, transpersonal coach, and author of *The Living Hanuman*).

A Ship
Of Many Oars

A Collection of Short Stories

NIRAJ SRIVASTAVA

PARTRIDGE
A Penguin Random House Company

To order additional copies of this book, contact
Partridge India
000 800 10062 62
orders.india@partridgepublishing.com

www.partridgepublishing.com/india

Contents

For Papa,
May the road rise up to meet you,
May the wind be always at your back,
The sun shine warm upon your face,
The rain fall soft upon your fields,
And until we meet again,
May God hold you in the hollow of HIS Hand.

An old Irish toast

Preface

Words do have wings—they have a life and a spring of their own. When used creatively, they can emote into a thousand beautiful thoughts and actions; when used destructively, they can tear apart whole nations, families, and the individual souls!

The author, like the potter, churns the stone of his words to reflect the rampaging thoughts of his restless mind. For him, as he churns alone, no sentence is good enough, no plot thick enough to entice his readers. He always strives for more—to give *his* best to the reader. And therein lies a story.

Immediately upon completion of my formal education, I was plunged into the demands of a very short but rewarding tenure with Remington Rand of USA and Jaypee Cements thereafter. Then came the hurly-burly of managing my own security service of more than 3,300 personnel (almost a brigade!) as well as business interests in education and real estate. This continued for almost two decades!

On the eve of my wife's birthday in July 2012, I asked her preference for a gift, and pat came her reply: 'Write me a story!' Thus, 'A Wondrous Star' was born, the first story in this anthology!

A Ship of Many Oars is a kaleidoscope of colourful events, time, and people who very closely resemble people we know, for reality does imitate fiction! Nawab Mian Muazzam Ali from 'The Nawab of Bilaul' is a quixotic character full of old-world charm and *tehzeeb*, and it is a loose imitation of my great-great-grandfather, late Rai Kali Prasad, who, in his happy inebriated state, *did* get into an ugly brawl with the British resident commissioner at Benares and *did* whip him with his chappals and hookah hose! We *did* pay dearly for his misdemeanour!

'24 South Road' is a fictitious wrangling of all that I witness inside a bank during their opening hours. I pray such stories never happen!

'Hostile Takeover' is a side-thumping satire on all that ails our society and *maybe* my suppressed desires. 'The Winding Road' is for an evening of spooky pakoras and chai!

My engagement with retired soldiers and JCOs of the Indian Army who joined my security service gave me ample opportunities to see their interactions at close quarters. Most of my supervisory and instructional staff were from the Rajput and Gorkha regiments, and thus happened 'Hukum Singh'!

'Exodus' was borne out of my own experiences. The perils of a yodeller range from the sublime to the absolutely malodorous! Read at your own peril!

'Travesty of Justice' is a sombre reminder of all that is vexatious about fate and its malicious ally, justice.

'The Hermit' is a historical fiction where history closely follows fiction and the ravines of Bundelkhand come alive to the cries of freedom. Reader, beware. History is not always what it seems!

In conclusion, this work is purely fictional, and any resemblance to any person, living or dead, is *deliberately* coincidental! And I, the author, am totally responsible for all omissions and remissions in text or judgement!

To weave a story, the writer has to get inside the *weft* and the *warp* to get the right *pick*! In my stories also, I have deliberately immersed myself into the situations and characters along with their idiosyncrasies and colourful vernacular! The stories and characters would not have come close to reality otherwise!

Happy reading!

Email: nirajsrivastava.author@gmail.com

Acknowledgements

As with every author, I owe the creation of this anthology of short stories to several people, places, time, and events that came together in my hands to weave these words into stories.

To all my friends, far and wide, I say thank you for being there for me. To my employees and staff, a big thank you for letting me write in peace and for managing without my breath on your necks! To my eyes, laptop, and fingers, I say thank you for surviving this ordeal with me and enjoying every minute of it!

A special word of praise to the publishing and editorial team at Partridge for their professional handling of a debut author! Their efficiency, courtesy, and turnaround time is truly amazing. Jeric Romano, my senior publishing consultant at Partridge, is an amazing guide—helpful, troubleshooter *extraordinaire*, and full of confidence in the prowess of his fledgling authors! Muchas gracias!

I am indebted to my friend Ranjit 'Dinky' Banerjee, executive vice president of A. H. Wheelers, for going out of his way to promote my meagre skills!

To Suhail Mathur, the bestselling author of the 'Bhairav Putras' and my new found friend, a major 'Thank You' for reading my stories in their raw manuscript form. It certainly is our Bhairav connection at work!

I shall forever be in debt to my father, late Dr Devendra Srivastava, who instilled in us (my sister, Nupur, and me) the good habit of reading and who never said no to any request of mine when it came to books, and to my mother for her silent smiles of encouragement.

I would not have ventured on this path had it not been for the constant exhortation of my beloved wife, Smita, and her gentle pressure (tortuous, at times!) to utilize my writing skills! This book is more hers than mine!

Thank you, Smita, for your fortitude in bearing with my testiness and churlish behaviour over the last two months as I worked on this anthology—I hope to make it up to you!

All the illustrations in this book have been done by her, and they add meaning to my words! Thank you!

I am grateful to my son, Devesh, and my daughter, Riticka, for accepting my long periods of silence even when they were home on short vacations. Their continuous grading of 8 to my writing skills made me carry on—9 is reserved for Ruskin Bond and J.K. Rowling!

This book and now my pursuit of writing are by Shree Batuk Bhairav's grace. None of this would have been possible without his blessings, for in Shree Bhairav Ashthak, it says, 'Vishal keerti dayakam.' Bestowing his devotees with legendary fame!

As I walked the desolate shores alone,
And shuddered at the thunderous roar,
Of the petulant and the stormy sea,
I knew there was a cloud above
To shield me from the burning rays,
And a cradle, in thine arms again!
For fate is nothing but a penny unspent,
And faith, the redeeming chapter!

And for my readers who have shown faith in my stories and have invested their valuable time and money, a heartfelt invocation for an enjoyable read!

Allahabad
14 July 2015

The Wondrous Star

Mohan and the donkey stared at each other with equal malevolence. It was difficult to ascertain who had the more intense glare.

Mohan sat on his charpoy with a dirty glass of home-made hooch and addressed his adversary, 'Do you think I am Shah Rukh Khan that you are staring at me? Now, move your royal presence from my sight before I get up and give a royal kick on your royal backside. Son of a pig!'

The donkey continued to gaze at Mohan, albeit with a little less malevolence. He wondered if Mohan had his anthropology right or had just made an ass of himself by getting his lineage twisted with a pig!

Mohan stared bleakly at the donkey and, getting no response except for the occasional swishing of his tail, heaved himself off the charpoy and landed a solid kick on the donkey's rump. He was instantly rewarded by a reverse kick of such magnitude that it left Mohan stretched on the ground, clasping his shin. To add insult to his grief, the donkey raised its tail and deposited a full plate of moist, steamy, malodorous intestinal debris flat on Mohan's face and chest.

It is said that his screams that night scared away all the evil spirits in the neighbourhood.

His wife, Ramleela, came rushing out to find Mohan screeching like a demented banshee—and worse, smelling like a putrid drain. She could not believe her eyes at the sight. Mohan was dripping with factory-fresh donkey waste with contorted lips and flailing arms!

She helped him to stand and steered him towards the municipal handpump, keeping well clear of the donkey, who was now evidently enjoying Mohan's new look. Mohan sat under the pump and gazed in alarm at the sky. 'This is the revenge of the gods,' moaned Mohan. 'I should not have said bad things! O Krishna, forgive me! I promise you that I will never ever call you a liar or a thief! I will bring you laddus every Tuesday. Do *not* punish me! O Krishna, forgive, forgive!'

Mohan's lamenting arose from the recent thrashing he had received at the hands of his neighbours when he tried to embellish his dinner with the neighbours' hen. The hen cackled and hopped around the yard till its owners came running to find Mohan mimicking the hen's action. Without much ado, Mohan found himself at the receiving end of fists, kicks, and a bamboo pole which kept searching for his posterior!

Then Mohan screamed heavenwards, 'O Krishna, lord of the universe, is this your justice? You have double standards, ha! One for yourself and one for poor mortals like me. You lived your life stealing milk and curd and clothes all across your village and beyond, and nobody said a word! They even made you a god! Oh, you sweet-tongued liar, you made a fool out of everyone, including me! I only tried to catch that mangy bird for my simple dinner, and you sent the whole village after me? And I could have shared it with you if you had asked! But now I will never see your face again, at least till the pain on my bottom subsides. Also, I will not bring you any sweets. You can go and try to steal the laddus now, and I hope the villagers catch you with that bamboo pole. Then you will understand how it feels to be decorated with a bamboo pole on the tender parts. I hope that wretched bird comes under the wheels of the garbage truck and Mangu, who struck me on my face with his smelly chappals, is loaded in the truck as well and unloaded in the deepest pits of Bhakru Nala!'

Mohan spent many days in dread after this outburst, fearing that maybe he had gone a bit too far and that Krishna might just decide to teach him a lesson by sending Hanumanji (on loan from Shri Ram) with his mace to tingle his backside again!

His reminiscing was broken by the sharp contact of water on his head, and he opened one eye (freshly cleaned of dung) to look at the skies and possibly to see if Krishna had forgiven him. From beneath the streams of water flowing over his eyes, he could see a star shining brightly. The star seemed to be winking at him. Mohan shook his head and plastered his wife with a cascade of dirty water. He looked again, and yes, the star was winking at him! He was about to abusively address the winking star for making fun of his misfortune when his wife exclaimed 'O Lord, see what I have found!'

Mohan opened both his eyes to see his wife holding a glittering object in her hand the size of a pencil eraser. He snatched it from her and peered at it closely—he could make out the letters—'99.99 % pure'. He quacked, 'Where did you find it?' Ramleela was sitting on her haunches and replied, 'It was inside the dung stuck on your neck. When I was scrubbing you, it fell on my palms. It is gold, is it not?' The quiver in her voice was evident.

'Yes, it is! Now we can live for the next ten years in comfort,' exclaimed Mohan.

He looked again towards the sky, folded his palms to the star which was shining more than the others, and mumbled, 'Thank you, O Krishna! You have truly forgiven me!'

The star winked and was gone.

Hostile Takeover

India (23.42 Hours)

There is a blinding flash and then searing, melting heat. Concrete structures, once proud and erect, touching the skies, are slowly melting unto themselves and settling into heaving, misshapen piles. Iron railings, supports, and structural links are burning along with automobiles and buses, which have been compressed into burning shells.

The citizens have been incinerated into bones and skulls, with small strips of burning flesh smouldering in radioactive rage.

The Indian cities of New Delhi, Agra, Jaipur, and Mumbai have ceased to exist. Satellites passing overhead are recording and transmitting live images of black debris and mushroom clouds over north India and midway on the western coastline of India, over a jutting strip of land.

The unthinkable has happened. Pakistan has nuked India. Within seconds, presidential hotlines are buzzing across the world, enabling voice scramblers and digital encoding for the world to act.

The doors to Armageddon have been opened.

Heaven, Celestial Chambers (23.44 Hours)

Almighty God is woken up by the incessant hammering on the doors of his celestial chamber.

'Come in,' he shouts, not at all happy with being interrupted in such a manner. He opens one eye to see his personal assistant, Narad Muni, standing with folded hands. He opens both his eyes and questions his PA with a raised brow.

'My lord, forgive this intrusion, but we have a tremendous influx of people from Earth, both here and in hell. It seems Pakistan has struck some parts of India with nuclear weapons, and we have almost 14 million souls trying to get into heaven and hell. Yamraj is asking for more hands to man the Pearly Gates. He is finding it difficult to issue relevant gate passes for heaven and hell to the right souls. All of them are demanding entry into heaven.'

'Tell Yamraj to put more staff for gate passes to hell—I am sure that 75 per cent of the souls are destined to be there. Make sure all the brawny, moustachioed, yamdoots are stationed on the hell desk. Ask a few apsaras to sacrifice their beauty sleep and man the heaven desk. I want the good souls to be received properly. Remember, first impressions are the last impressions. And, Narad, do not ever bang on the door again—it reminds me of Manjolika. If there is anything urgent, call on the Sancharnet. It seems to be working today.'

Narad Muni furrows his brows—he thought he knew every secret and gossip in the three worlds, but who was this Manjolika? As he bows his way out of the celestial chambers, he decides to find out once this crisis is over.

Celestial Secretariat (00.08 Hours)

The chimes on the black cell phone denote a call from hell. A dozing Narad picks up the phone only to come suddenly awake at the stern tone in Yamraj's voice. 'Narad Dev, please send me more doots at the hell desk. There seems to be an overflow of souls destined for hell. I am totally understaffed, and these idiots thronging the desk are making it difficult for me and my staff to operate. They are trying to crawl under the table and are suddenly popping up between our legs, demanding VIP passes. Our dhotis have almost come undone many times when their heads become entangled in the folds. I might just kick a few of them soon if they don't settle down.'

'Calm down, O lord of death. All will be fine in a few celestial seconds. I am sending more staff to you, but where is your army of *yamdoot*s, my lord?' queries Narad as he tries to dial the HR department for extra staff.

'I had to send half of them to hell to bring some order there. I was informed that there is a fierce fight going on down there for the best seats. Some of them are waving some kind of SC/ST/OBC certificate and claiming reservation. Their leader seems to be a fat lady with short hair who has pulled up a chair in front of mine and was telling me to sit on the floor in front of her. She said that all her people, including her MLAs and MPs, do not dare sit on a chair in her presence. The bloody cheek of her! When I told her there is no reservation or quota system in hell, she was threatening to flood hell with statues of elephants and her own grand self! Why don't you call her to heaven, Narad Dev?'

'No, thank you. We have enough statues and fountains in heaven. And, Yamraj-ji, please leave this habit of trying to pass all your problems to us! Now let me arrange extra staff for you. Goodnight.'

Seething with rage and swearing to put Narad Muni on the back of his bullock for a ride through the three worlds once this crisis was over, Yamraj clouts a fat male on his head as he tries to extricate himself from between the folds of Yamraj's dhoti.

Pearly Gates, Celestial Secretariat, Celestial Palace and Chambers (01.24 Hours)

Narad Muni is plugged into Sonic News and is fast scrolling the Search menu for God's discomfiture with Manjolika. Ah, there it is—a small news snippet that God had terrible convulsions upon watching a performance of the song 'Mera Dholna . . . Aami je tomar' during a private screening of the Bollywood movie *Bhool Bhulaiya* and had taken a pathological hatred to the ghostly dancer Manjolika in the movie. *Oh-ho*, thought Narad, *this explains God's admonition regarding this wretched Manjolika!*

The golden cell phone rings. Narad Dev sighs happily and picks up the hotline from Pearly Gates. The agitated voice of Lord Brihaspat explodes in Narad Muni's unsuspecting ears. 'Naradji, I wish to speak to the Almighty. Now!'

Naradji tries to pacify him. 'Dev Guru Brihaspat, I am sorry, but the lord is resting and does not wish to be disturbed. But, guruji, what are you doing at the gates? Where is Yamraj-ji? Can I help you, sire?'

Lord Brihaspat, with his voice shaking like his white beard, exclaims, 'Yamraj had to leave for hell. His doots were heavily outnumbered and were getting clobbered by the wild crowd there. The yamdoot who brought the news had had his moustache torn off—said that some Bollywood costume wallah snatched it for his next film! Yamraj was almost in tears when he heard how his doots were hiding behind rocks and crevices. Some of them had even rubbed soot on to their nice clothes and body to merge with the cretins there and escape the wrath of the new entrants! Look, Narad, I called because I need the good lord to intervene here. I am having a terrible time. Please wake him up.'

Narad can not deny the wishes of Lord Brihaspat, the guru of all devas, and patches a call through to the celestial chambers. God picks up on the first ring.

'What is it, Narad? I had a feeling you would call me soon.'

'Sire, Guru Brihaspat is on conference call from the Pearly Gates. He insisted on speaking to you.'

'Put him through.'

'Forgive me, lord, for disturbing you. But I am about to faint. There is this swarthy small man with a funny voice, calls himself Manna Bazaare, with a white topi on his head. He is insisting that his soul is as clean as his white kurta and wants direct entry into heaven. And, sire, his kurta is not all that clean! He is challenging me to meet him at some place called Jantar Mantar. Sire, please direct Guru Shukra to handle him. He is the one into Jantar Mantar of all types, not me!'

God jauntily replies, 'O learned sage, did you not tell him that we will throw him in hell if he does not stop his blabbering?'

Guru Brihaspat almost weeps. 'I did, sire. But he has three or four chamchas surrounding him who are urging him to go on indefinite hunger strike. He was about to take off his kurta and squat in the middle of the road when I begged him to hold on. We can't have hunger strikes in heaven, can we, sire? One of the chamchas is a lady with cropped hair who started demanding a permit to hold a rally in heaven as their last one went up in nuclear smoke a few hours ago. I told her I cannot help her, but she is frightening me by reciting sections of something called IPC and CrPC and is threatening to implicate me in a child molestation case if I don't help her. Sire, I am a *brahmachari*. What must I do?'

'Let me think . . .'

'Lord, it gets worse. They have been joined by a man in saffron half dhoti with a dyed beard and a bun at the back of his neck. Others are calling him Baba Kamdeo. He looks like an original shipwreck! He is sitting in front of the apsaras and twitching his left eye at them. I have caught the twitch also in my left eye, and I can't help but twitch! He is selling some kind of powder to the apsaras and assuring them that they will also start twitching in the right anatomical areas after using this powder. Sire, do something, or I will twitch myself to death,' says a weeping Brihaspat.

'Gurudev, calm down. I will send Hanuman to teach these fellows a lesson,' replies God, his ire rising.

'It will not work, sire. I saw Hanumanji running away from here a few minutes ago. The new entrants here were trying to bribe Hanumanji into doing a repeat performance of his Lanka sojourn by burning his tail. When he refused, they started reciting different *chalisa*s to please him. A few rogues tried to tie firecrackers on his tail. Hanumanji fled. He said to tell you that he cannot live through another tail-burning!'

'And, sire . . .' God can hear great heaving sobs. 'Sire, Aham Sharnagat, save me, please. There are a group of people calling themselves Bollywood actors, shirtless and characterless, chasing all the apsaras around trees. Get your hands off me, you scoundrel! Not you, sire . . . There is this villainous-looking fellow who is trying to pull me down on a couch. Get lost, you lech. I don't want your couch benefits, whatever they might be! Forgive me, sire, he wants a threesome. I don't understand one word of his.' Guru Brihaspat is weeping like a child.

'Great sage, do not cry. I am sending one-half of my celestial army to help you, and the other half, I shall be sending to Yamraj. All will be well.' God instructs his PA to do the needful.

Mt Kailash (Lord Shiva's HQ), Celestial Secretariat (03.40 Hours)

Narad Dev is staring gloomily at his veena when the videoconferencing CLED screen comes alive. Naradji quails as the glowering face of Lord Shiva comes into focus from Mt Kailash. His third eye has not yet opened but is glowing an angry red.

'My lord.' Narad bows.

'Sage Narad,' thunders Lord Shiva, 'you better tell the imbeciles trying to control hell to find and punish a fellow with slicked-back dyed hair, thick-rimmed sunglasses, wearing ochre robes. He is calling himself Kaal Bhagaley and roaring like a lion. You tell your army to find him fast, or I shall come down myself and give a taste of my *trishul* on their lazy backsides. Do you understand?'

Narad Muni has never seen Lord Shiva in such a towering rage. 'May I ask the reason for your displeasure, my lord?' Narad mumbles, not daring to look up at the ferocious visage on the screen.

'This imposter is sitting on a big machan, surrounded by dozens of his lazy scoundrels, and they are calling themselves Shiv Doots. The lying lot! They will not even become sweepers in my army if they ever apply. They will spread mutiny and rot in my army. They are already sending oily scallywags to recruit more rotten hordes. If that joker even looks towards Mt Kailash and my army, I swear on my trishul, I will send Bhairava to put his Dand up their rotten backsides. And I will skin the joker alive! And you too, Narad! You better act before I react!'

Narad opens one eye fearfully to see the terrible image of a teeth-gnashing Shiva fade from the screen.

As he picks up the black cell phone to hell to order the arrest of this supercilious joker and his phoney army, Naradji promises himself that he will put in his VRS application on medical grounds first thing in the morning. He cannot survive another night like this—the peptic ulcers in his stomach are telling him.

Celestial Chambers, Celestial Secretariat, Hell, Heaven, Pearly Gates (04.05 Hours)

The golden phone from Pearly Gates rings on Naradji's desk. Naradji continues weeping. The phone rings again, and Naradji picks it up after wiping his tears and snotty nose. 'Hello.' He weeps into the phone.

'Narad, help me. My life is in danger. There is this group of industrialists from Mumbai who are demanding air-conditioned offices. I told them that heaven does not need air-conditioning, but they are not listening. They are joined by some demented politicians and bureaucrats who want a transfer to hell. They are saying there is no scope for scams in heaven—their talents here will be wasted. On my refusal, they are planning on giving a *supari* on my life! Oh, I will resign from my position as guru deva! See here, I have been forwarded a petition from hell of some politicians who want to carve out their constituencies as per their vote banks! We do not have a ghetto culture! And what will happen to poor Yamraj? Please wake up God before I . . .' Brihaspat sputters into the phone.

The black cell phone from hell rings. Narad picks it up and, fearing the worst, says softly, 'Yes, Yamraj-ji . . .'

'Lord, it is not Maharaj Yamraj,' cries a baritone in extreme grief. 'I am his yamdoot, Bhaukali. How can I tell you, sire . . . Maharaj is hiding in the loo.'

'What! The lord of death is hiding in a toilet? Hold on, I am putting God on conference call. Sage Brihaspat, you also stay on the line.'

'My life is on the line, and you are telling me to stay on the line? Hey, Bhagwan, save me.'

'Yes,' answers God to be immediately assaulted by the warbling cries of Bhaukali. 'My lord and god, it is terrible. Maharaj Yamraj is seeking shelter inside a toilet. He was chased by a group of scientists from Trombay who wanted to launch Maharaj Yamraj and us yamdoots into Pakistan. Said it was better than nuking them. Lord, all the yamdoots have also gone underground.'

'Shit, this is too much!' Such language from sage Brihaspat is unthinkable. 'My *gandharvas* are getting beaten up by a bunch of hoodlums calling themselves the indie rockers. Shit, look at their smelly clothes and bulging arms.' There is no stopping Brihaspat now. 'One of them just wrapped a celestial harp around the neck of my favourite gandharva. There goes our music! F—, one of them has laid a good-looking gandharva on his lap and is trying to strum him. F— all *ragi* is being beaten on his head with half-torn boots. What *taal* is that? F— me, they have caught Meneka and are making her do a lap dance. Kill me first, you louts!'

'Lord . . .' The anguished wail of Bhaukali singes God's ear. 'These f— have caught hold of Lord Kuber and are demanding a ransom. They are demanding dollars, not rupees, shit. Why did you put that broom up my arse? Sorrrrry . . . Sire, there is this fat Bengali lady in a crumpled, dirty sari with bulging eyes. Yes, yes, she is the one with the broom up my bottom. She is wanting to be quartered with Netaji Bose in heaven. Says all Sonar Bengalis together. F—, don't twist the broom. Oh, she is threatening to do the same to you. Forgive me, lord, I have a bad case of piles. Mother, don't shove it so hard. She is wanting your address and wanting to know if it is close to 10 Janpath . . . Padyatra. Says she will kick us all out of heaven like she has kicked numerous others.'

'Sire,' Narad's frantic voice cuts through. 'Yamraj has put his crown for sale on eBay. F——, it seems he is joined by 3.3 million more devis and devas selling their crowns.'

The sound of divine wailing rents the air.

'Enough! thunders God.

Celestial Chambers (04.40 Hours)

Narad Muni is holding on to the lord's leg as he thrashes violently on the celestial bed. Narad is sure that God has suffered an epileptic fit.

He beseeches, 'Lord, wake up. Shesh Naag is finding it difficult to keep his one thousand heads over water. He is complaining of water and weeds in his nostrils with you thrashing about so wildly. Wake up, lord!'

Vikas Puri, New Delhi (04.41 Hours)

Sandy Mathur's flatmate enters the room to see him thrashing around on the bed and trying to pull weeds out of his nostrils. Wasting no time, he picks up a glass of cold water and pours it upon his face. 'Wake up, Sandy, wake up! And stop thrashing around like a gorilla in labour. Stop dreaming! Get up and fill the buckets. The water will vanish at 5 a.m.'

Sandy Mathur sits up groggily in bed and yells, 'Call Narad!'

Another jug of cold water descends on his face and elevates him straight into the bathroom.

Bye-bye, dreams!

24 South Road

The bank had opened to customers—as usual, at 10 a.m. sharp. A few early customers and a couple of employees being chronic latecomers had just walked into the bank. The early morning chasm between hyperactivity and languor was evident in the sluggish pace of its employees.

The two guards on duty, having replaced the night shift at 8 a.m., were at their morning best, greeting each customer and employee with a cheery 'Good morning, saar!' Deena Nath, the older of the two, was a retired subedar from the Grenadiers, and at fifty-two, he considered himself to be the self-appointed counsellor to all the class 4 employees of the bank. The peons and maintenance personnel also suffered his counselling in silence as they were rewarded with a glass of tea and a free smoke. Clean shaven and smiling, with the beginnings of a paunch, Deena Nath was much liked by the bank officials and the customers.

Sukh Deo Singh, on the other hand, was a huge barrel-chested fellow with well-oiled curly moustaches and gimlet eyes. He had just retired from the Jat Regiment and was given re-employment by the Army Resettlement Board. Unlike Deena Nath, he kept his double-barrelled shotgun in his hands, barrel pointing down, as he surveyed each customer with suspicion. He preferred to stand in a far corner, diagonally opposite from the tellers' cabins. Unsmiling and friendless, Sukh Deo Singh was an anomaly in the friendly atmosphere of this branch.

The branch manager, Urvashi Singh, a management graduate with six to seven years of service in this bank, was resigned to facing another day of routine banking. She glanced at her branch colleagues through her glass partition and saw them settling down and the initial flickering of their computer screens. She looked at her cell phone with despair, waiting for it to buzz with the daily morning conference call from her immediate superior sitting at Lucknow. These con calls were an indescribable pain in the ass, she mused as she waited for the same invocations to come with dreamt-up targets. 'Increase your sales of insurance policies. You are lagging behind all the other branches. Your collections in savings need to get better. Go easy on the current accounts. Your office expenses are hitting the roof. Have you become a coffee-vending machine? Seventy-eight cups of coffee in a day? And listen, the mother of the regional head, Mr Suhag would be visiting sangam on Wednesday. Arrange for an air-conditioned taxi and accompany her there. I guess the pandas give a hard time to first-timers. And pay it from your pocket. We can adjust the expenses over the week from Staff Welfare.'

Urvashi grimaced at the thought of sangam. Everyone—from her bank's chairman to the assistant manager, accompanied by his pet Labrador—had visited sangam, the holy confluence of the mighty Ganges, Yamuna, and the mythical Saraswati! With everyone washing their sins there, the waters were as polluted (or maybe more!) as any other river. She often wondered if she should quit her bank career and turn into a bottler and supplier of 'pure, sangam waters . . . guaranteed to rid you of all your accumulated sins!' She would send a complimentary bottle to all her seniors to absolve them of their daily sins of setting unachievable targets and unwarranted rebukes.

Her morose musing was broken by the discordant buzz of her cell. The screen lit up with the words 'ulcer agent' as she reached out for another con call.

*   *   *

Today was Tuesday, and the operations manager and the senior cashier were busy in getting the four huge iron trunks secured by chains and special locks designed by Leahy & Co., Ireland. These locks, with almost seventeen levers, were able to withstand direct hammer blows. The collection over the weekend from the branch's main customers, the shops, and showrooms of posh Civil Lines deposited on Monday would now be collected by the Cash Management Agency for deposit at the mother branch. The cash collection van was expected in half an hour.

'Narottamji, have you put in the bait money?'

'Yes, sir. The Rs.500/- bundles are in three chests, and a Rs.100/- bundle is in the fourth chest.'

'Good,' replied Sarvesh Singh, the branch operations manager.

The four chests containing Rs.3.28 crores were dragged into the anteroom. Sarvesh Singh busied himself with the paperwork regarding cash transfer as the senior cashier made his way to the inward cash teller counter. Today, the inward cash window was manned by Narottam Shukla, and the outward cash remittance window was being handled by Mr Rajendra Yadav, one of the oldest employees of the bank, with almost thirty-two years of uninterrupted service behind him.

Mr Yadav was happiest at the inward remittance window, where he would happily count, with utmost glee, the cash being deposited in his beloved branch. With his experienced fingers, he would check and then double-, triple-check any currency note which he did not like. If still not satisfied, he would put the note against the ceiling CFL tube and squint. He had not much belief in the cash counting and counterfeit detecting machine installed just to his left. 'Arre, woh machine hi to hai!' he would say when questioned by the irate customers waiting to deposit. It is only a machine!

If for any reason Mr Yadav was ever deputed to the cash outward window, his face would be a mask of anguish as he counted out the money to withdrawing customers. Whenever a large withdrawal was made, Yadav Saheb would agonize over the departing cash and would let go with such sorrow that the customer would feel relieved at the passage of currency into his hands and would scuttle out from the bank premises at full speed.

Ashwani, one of the two bank peons, was busy refilling the pay-in slips, withdrawal forms, insurance brochures, and other leaflets stacked on two shelves for the customers' convenience. Nemai Chand, the other peon, was walking around with glasses of cold water.

Outside, on the street, a municipal worker with a wheelbarrow was collecting trash, while another worker with a wheelbarrow looked idly on.

*   *   *

Deena Nath looked up at the big round wall clock—10.25 a.m. *Good*, he thought, *time for the morning cup of tea!* In expectation of the steaming brew, he shifted the shotgun to a more comfortable position on his shoulder.

The glass doors swung open, and three neatly dressed youngsters walked in. Deena Nath smiled at them as he had seen them on a number of previous visits. One of them, dressed in blue jeans and a checked shirt, approached the inward cash counter, where Mr Yadav was sitting.

'I wanted to open an account here. Whom should I meet?'

Mr Yadav, unhappy with not receiving any cash from this early morning customer, considered it an ill omen and irritably pointed towards the junior officer's enclosure. As he turned his head, he was astounded to see Deena Nath and Sukh Deo Singh both disarmed and silently being pushed into a corner, prodded by the blackened steel barrels of revolvers.

Suddenly the two persons masquerading as municipal workers also barged in with sawn-off shotguns, which they had concealed in their wheelbarrows. The wheelbarrows were now tightly wedged against the bank's entrance to dissuade entry. A yellow dilapidated sign 'Work in progress' was prominently displayed in the centre.

One of them ran into the manager's cabin while the other person urged the stupefied customers to gather together near the far wall. The two robbers, who had entered with blue jeans, had by now tied and gagged the two guards, and for good measure, they had clouted both of them across their temples with revolver butts. Bleeding and helplessly tied, the pain and shame was evident in Deena Nath's and Sukh Deo's eyes.

*   *   *

Urvashi looked up with some irritation at the intrusion and was instantly dealt a blow to her jaw, which left her sprawled on the floor. Her cell phone flew from her hands and alighted a few feet away. From the speaker, the voice of her accursed senior kept rasping, 'Urvashi, what happened? Speak up. I can't hear you. Speak up!'

She was pulled up roughly by her hand, and in a menacing voice, the robber said, 'Do not touch anything, just come out quietly. No, don't touch your mobile.'

Urvashi desperately wanted to touch the silent alarm in the footwell of her desk, but how would she do it now?

She held on to the edge of her desk as if she was about to faint, and weaving sporadically, she crashed on to the floor. With lightning speed, her fingers pressed the alarm button located on the right side of the footwell, which gave a tiny buzz, signalling activation. Relieved, she pushed herself to her hands and knees and stood up. She moved forward towards the door with a hand covering her mouth as if about to puke.

Meanwhile, Blue Jeans gestured for Mr Yadav to get out of his cubicle along with Narottam and join the other employees. Yadav looked down and tried to push his feet into his shoes—he had a disgusting habit of taking off his shoes and locking his feet behind his chair's legs.

'You move your fucking leg, and I will blow your fucking brains out,' hissed Blue Jeans as he swiped Yadav across his mouth with the revolver. 'Just come out now.'

It was 10.28 a.m. now.

Two robbers moved towards Urvashi and hit her in the abdomen with their balled fists. As she doubled up with pain, she heard Blue Jeans ask, 'Where are the cash trunks?'

No answer.

This time, she received a flurry of punches to her face. Urvashi screamed with pain and reeled back as she tried to cover her face with her hands.

'This time, I will put a bullet in your belly. Tell me, where is it?'

'In the next room,' quivered Narottam, horrified by the beating he had just witnessed of a woman.

Blue Jeans pushed Narottam ahead and, with two more accomplices, went into the anteroom. The two criminals who were now left in the main lobby became more alert and raised their weapons.

It was 10.30 now.

Sardar Sukhwinder Singh, owner of a furniture shop in Civil Lines, had come to deposit cash in the bank. As he was on diuretics, he had frequent urges to urinate and, on entering the branch, had made straight for the washroom. The deposit could wait for later.

As he opened the door, he heard a female scream and saw the bank manager Urvashi Singh being hit by fists across her face. Quickly he eased the door closed and bolted it from inside. With his heart thudding, he brought the small cloth bag filled with cash closer to his chest. *Thank God for diuretics*, he prayed.

He took out his cell phone and dialled 100, the police emergency number. After what seemed an interminable wait, the phone was picked up. 'Police control room,' said a tobacco-chewing voice.

'Sir, I am calling from Garuda Bank, Civil Lines. There is a dacoity going on here,' whispered Sukhwinder.

'State your name and address.'

'Sir, there is a dacoity in progress. My name is Sardar Sukhwinder Singh, and the bank is located on South Road, Civil Lines, near Fire Brigade.'

'What is *your* address?'

'*Ullu de patthe* [son of an owl]! My address is your mother's pussy! There is a fucking dacoity going on here!' hissed a seething Sardar Sukhwinder Singh as he disconnected the phone and started dialling his wife to apprise her and to ask her to dial others and the police control to signify the gravity of the crime happening before his eyes.

He was about to dial when he heard the sound of something heavy being dragged.

He froze.

*   *   *

The operator in the control room, disconcerted by the sardar's temerity in abusing him via his 'mother's pussy', looked at the black telephone receiver with distaste. In the police operator's eyes, only the police had a monopolistic right to abuse by and large—or maybe some uncouth politicians!

Spitting the tobacco out with a practised turn of his head, he muttered a few of his choicest expletives at the invisible sardar and then picked up the wireless transmitter.

'Police control to Thana Civil Lines, emergency . . . Come in.'

His transceiver squawked, 'Thana Civil Lines, go ahead, control.'

'Reported dacoity in progress at Garuda Bank Civil Lines near fire brigade. Respond immediately. Code 3,' intoned the police control operator. Repeat, code 3.'

Bank robberies were awarded the highest emergency code—except code red, which was reserved for an assassination attempt on a VVIP.

Following protocol, the police operator patched the call on a live feed with the nearest cruising Innova interceptor as well as the superintendent and senior superintendent of police.

'Romeo 12, come in. Code 3 alert,' intoned the senior operator known as Ustad in the control room. He had taken control of this loop now, considering its implicit gravity.

Romeo 12, the designated Innova interceptor, was standing under the shade of a peepul tree near AG office crossing, and the sub-inspector with three constables manning the interceptor was standing outside, productively engaged in watching the passing traffic. An enterprising constable was busy bargaining for guavas with a roadside vendor. The sub-inspector yawned and wiped his face with his sleeve. He glanced towards the guavas and decided they were not good enough to warrant his intervention.

It was now 10.35 a.m.

Having dragged the four trunks into the bank lobby, the armed criminals pushed the employees and the few customers into the anteroom. Mr Yadav, the cashier, was at the end of his tether, watching all that cash being taken away. He suddenly saw Blue Jeans' mobile screen light up with an incoming call. Distracted by the call, Blue Jeans looked at his buzzing cell phone and barked, 'Later!'

Mr Yadav, seizing this momentary distraction, lunged at Blue Jeans, who managed to sidestep and whipped his pistol across Mr Yadav's face. One of the criminals standing to the side stepped up and kicked the cashier as he lay sprawled on the floor. Then they dragged him inside the anteroom and locked him up with the others.

Dragging the four trunks outside, the criminals heaped them on to the wheelbarrows and trundled them across the twenty yards of pavement to where their Maruti Eeco van was standing with its sliding doors open. The few onlookers were too startled to observe or say anything. The doors closed, and the van eased into the traffic.

It was now 10.38 a.m.

'Romeo 4, moving now. ETA four minutes.'

'Good, Romeo 4. This is Tiger. Moving now.'

'Tiger, Panther is already on the move.'

'Copy. Proceed.'

Tiger and Panther were the mobile codes for the senior superintendent of police and the superintendent of police (city) respectively.

'Fox Bravo, this is police control. Code 3 alert. Robbery in progress at Garuda Bank, 24 South Road. Very close to you. Reach immediately. Acknowledge.'

'Control, this is Fox Bravo. Copy code 3, Garuda Bank, South Road—'

Before the sentence was completed, the police dispatcher heard the sound of a siren in the background. As usual, the fire brigade were responding with alacrity.

Ustad, on his own initiative, had patched the fire brigade (Fox Bravo) as he was aware of their close proximity to Garuda Bank.

'Good work, control,' messaged Tiger, who was now holding the car's transceiver.

Sub-inspector Pandey, in charge of Romeo 12, frowned as he heard a babble of excited voices from the wireless transceiver installed within. Ducking his head inside, he caught the words 'code 3 alert, robbery in progress at Garuda Bank, 24 South Road'.

Shit. Fuck. Shit. Bank dacoity on his beat? He threw himself inside the vehicle and thumped on the door. All three constables turned to look and, seeing the stricken face of their leader, jumped inside the Innova.

'Romeo 12 proceeding to South Road,' croaked the sub-inspector as Arun Singh the constable driver revved up the engine and sped towards South Road with his roof-mounted strobe lights flashing and sirens wailing.

'Romeo 12, why were you not responding for—'

The police dispatcher's voice was cut as the SSP cut in, 'Romeo 12, this is Tiger. Were you washing your bloody backsides for the last half an hour? Who is in charge?'

'Jai Hind, saar. Sub-inspector Pandey, saar.'

'You better have a good explanation ready, Pandey, or face suspension,' growled the SSP.

It was now 10.44 a.m.

The fire brigade jeep was the first to arrive. They saw a crowd of people just outside the bank. The fire officer got down and shouted, 'What happened?'

'Dacoity,' came the chorus.

The fire officer, acutely aware that every minute could mean the fair divide between success and failure, immediately radioed, 'Dacoity confirmed. Repeat, dacoity confirmed.'

Unarmed as they were, the firemen rushed towards the bank's entrance. There was a blare of siren, and the first police vehicle, Romeo 4, arrived.

The firemen found two or three people trying to cut loose the binds on the guards. Apparently, after the criminals' hasty departure, a few brave souls had ventured inside the branch and had found the two guards bleeding and tied in a corner. There was no one else in the bank. And now, the fire and police personnel were here.

It was 10.45 a.m.

'Control, this is Tiger. Advise Sierra Oscar Civil Lines cantonment and Katra to rush to site. Initiate Vajra action. Panther, relay cordoning of all exit points. Now!'

'Copy.'

'All units, this is control. Enforce Vajra code. Repeat, enforce Vajra code. Acknowledge.'

The SP (city) radioed in, 'This is Panther. Advise all pickets and mobiles to man roadblocks. Bank robbery. Check and stop on suspicion. Armed and dangerous.'

Code Vajra was the action plan for overt police presence and action, akin to a flag march. It entailed the display and conspicuous presence of armed might. Police personnel and vehicles, on extra alert, were openly deputed at street corners, public places, and sensitive areas. Weapons were much in evidence as police stations (thanas) put extra force on the streets with weapons issued from the thana's *maalkhana* (quarter guard). The police wireless net sputtered with the heavy traffic of messages being relayed.

It was 10.47 a.m.

The last knot was undone, and the guards were set free. Immediately Sukh Deo stammered and, pointing towards the anteroom, said, 'The others are in there.'

A flurry of blows to the arms of the lock and the door flew open. A canvas of distended rolling eyes and mewling sounds greeted the police. The robbers had taken the trouble to lightly gag the employees and customers with broad surgical tape and had bound their hands and feet by simply passing and knotting a thick nylon cord along their wrists and ankles.

As the employees staggered out, a few of them started crying. Urvashi Singh, racked with pain from blows to her abdomen and face, looked silently around, with eyes brimming with unshed tears. A few customers tried to stand but collapsed on the floor again. Gently they were led to sit on the plastic seats in the lobby. Mr Narottam sat silently on a chair and cursed his fate. Why his branch of all the 220-odd branches available for plunder?

The door to the gents' toilet opened a fraction of an inch, and one eye, like a rolling bandicoot, checked the surroundings. Out went Sardar Sukhwinder Singh chanting, 'Wahe Guru, Wahe Guru.' A score of weapons were instantly turned on him.

Enraged, the Sikh growled, 'Imbeciles, idiots, am I a dacoit? Are you bloody insane?'

Slowly the weapons were lowered and revolvers holstered. Urvashi intervened, 'He is our customer. I hope you are all right, Singh Saheb.'

The ruffled Sikh was in no mood to back off and, looking directly at the SSP and SP (city), rasped, 'I called 100 while the robbery was in progress. The paan-chewing moron who answered my call was more interested in my name and address instead of the robbery. I will put my sword to his neck if I ever find him.'

The senior police officers exchanged glances as all the assembled people looked at them with accusing eyes.

Mr Rajendra Yadav sat, cupping his chin with his hands, oblivious to the bleeding cut on his temple. *Could so much happen in just thirteen minutes?* he mused. He looked around and saw only weeping, despairing faces.

The clamour of sirens and intense activity outside on the road was seeping into the catacomb-like atmosphere of the bank.

The SSP, Jaswant Singh (IPS, batch of 2006) was surveying the premises with a practised eye. The manager, a young woman of only about thirty years, was still in shock, but questions and time could not wait.

He walked up to her and asked, 'Madam, please sit down. I hate to rush you, but can you give a description of the robbers?'

*   *   *

Next morning, all the major and minor dailies prominently displayed the banner headline: 'Bank Dacoity in Daylight! 3.28 Crores Gone in 12 Minutes!' Smaller captions informed: 'No Clues; CCTV Compromised'.

The stories, with various embellishments, continued to describe in graphic detail the barbaric beating given to the branch head, Ms Urvashi Singh, the heroic lunge by Mr Rajendra Yadav, and the valiant withdrawal of Sardar Sukhwinder Singh to the Pacific climes of the men's washroom!

CCTV, normally the biggest deterrent to any robbery, had been compromised as the feed from live cameras had been put into a loop of a redundant video feed of almost two months back. It suggested the connivance of somebody from the bank or its security system vendor.

The police spokesman confirmed the above and said, 'It was a well-planned dacoity, with the active connivance of somebody from inside the bank.'

The branch manager and employees failed to give any satisfactory excuses to their security lapses and negligence.

*   *   *

Two days later, 11 a.m., Regent Mall, Lucknow

The ground floor of Regent Mall was just coming alive as the early shoppers and boys and girls on unauthorized furlough from their schools arrived. The central air-conditioning had just been switched on, and fresh notes of lavender wafted through the vents as maintenance sprayed the first of the six daily perfumed blasts into the cooling tower.

The semblance of commercial activity had yet to set in as shop owners were busy propitiating gods to bring cash and customers in and to keep the labour tax, sales tax, income tax, and police officials away. The gods, enervated by the clouds of incense smoke enveloping them, resigned themselves to another day of long harangue with mortals and their spiritual contractors!

The maintenance people, glowing like fireflies in their orange overalls, busily rode their electric mop carts along the floor and alleys of the mall. Security personnel were being briefed by their supervisors and were testing their handheld metal detectors.

Suddenly seven burly men converging from different directions rushed into the barely opened Jolly Café. While two of them, with drawn mini carbines, stood at the entrance, the others surrounded two young men having coffee.

Senior Inspector Manoj Yadav of the Special Operations Group (SOG), UP Police, caught one of them from behind the neck and banged his head on the table. His immediate junior, Inspector Rakesh Singh, had his arm around the neck and dragged him backwards on to the floor. Two others stepped up and, twisting their arms behind their backs, handcuffed them.

The shouts of protests from the apprehended men were swiftly dealt with heavy blows to the head and abdomen.

Gripping them by their arms, the SOG men half dragged and half pushed them across the lobby into an unmarked police Tavera. Moving swiftly away, the Tavera was joined by three more vehicles, all unmarked but with sinister-looking men inside. The backup team, which was securing the service entry at the rear of the mall, ran around to their unmarked Mahindra Scorpios and, with temporary flashing lights placed on their roofs, tore out of the mall parking.

'Lucknow control, this is Sierra Tango, Allahabad. Arrested two. Give us safe passage on Rae Bareli route.'

Lucknow police, which had already been briefed that a special team (Sierra Tango) from Allahabad was in town on a possible arrest, wasted no time in clearing the request.

'Lucknow control to Sierra Tango, Allahabad. You have safe passage. Traffic Zulu 3 on Abdul Hamid crossing. Provide escort to Allahabad Sierra Tango. Confirm.'

'Control, Zulu 3. Copy.'

The traffic interceptors were converted Innovas with supercharged engines and codenamed Zulus. Zulu 3, stationed at Shaheed Abdul Hamid crossing, swung on to the main road. As the sounds of several sirens reached the crossing, Zulu 3 emerged into the traffic. The motorcade of seven SUVs fell in behind the Innova as it cut a swathe in front with the incessant bark of its siren.

Normal police vehicles had sirens with their typical ululating wail but not the Zulus! Their sirens had short, sharp blasts which sounded like the rasping cough of a hyena in distress.

On the police wireless net, all police stations en route were being briefed about the dangerous convicts under transport. This meant a special vigil would be maintained all through the route to Allahabad as the concerned police precincts would ensure trouble-free movement of the police convoy in their jurisdiction. Similar police action took place in Fatehpur and the localities of Kydganj and Daraganj at Allahabad.

*   *   *

Allahabad, Third Day, 12.30 p.m.

The waiting hall of the SSP's office was packed with reporters and cameramen vying with one another to get vantage positions. A makeshift dais had been made at one end of the room, with several chairs and tables being placed. A solitary microphone stood next to a vase of roses.

Flashbulbs popped as the SSP, Jaswant Singh, strode into the room and took the central chair. Flanking him on both sides were SP (city) Anand Behari Rai and SOG senior inspector, Manoj Yadav.

'Good afternoon. This press conference has been called as we are happy to announce that the Garuda Bank dacoity has been solved, and culprits arrested. Stolen money has also been recovered.'

There was a babble of voices as each reporter threw his question at the police officers.

The SSP continued, 'Senior Inspector Manoj Yadav of SOG and his team were able to nab the criminals within forty-eight hours. Of the 3.28 crores stolen, we have recovered 3.22 crores. Our special thanks to Kolkata police and Lucknow police for their cooperation. We would also like to thank BSNL, Airtel, and Reliance for their unstinted support.'

The SSP made a slight gesture, and six men with manacles were pushed into the room with beefy, muscular men in plain clothes standing behind them.

Flashlights exploded as the reporters and cameramen craned to get a better view. The criminals tried to hide their faces by burying them into their chests, but a few well-placed fists in their kidneys and hissed instructions from their strapping keepers had them sullenly looking into the whirring cameras.

'Let me introduce the star cast to you,' sarcastic words came from Jaswant Singh. 'This man in blue jeans is the mastermind. His name is Ravi Gupta. A diploma holder in electronics. He hails from Katra area.'

All eyes were on Ravi Gupta as he stood there in his favourite blue jeans and checked shirt. Unshaven and unkempt, he looked more like a street vendor than a criminal genius.

'The others are, left to right, Ajay Singh from Deoria, residing at Allahpur, Durgesh Pandey from Fatehpur, Sohrab Khan from Kydganj, Babloo Lala from Daraganj. And the sixth person is the bank peon, Ashwani.'

He paused to study his notes and then continued, 'The seventh person, the driver of the getaway vehicle, Amar Singh from Sadar, was shot dead this morning in an exchange of fire with a police raiding party.'

Everyone was looking at these flawed humans—six of them, standing in a row, with churlish and surly expressions! Only Durgesh Pandey, tall and lanky, was sweeping the room with hostile eyes.

'Sir, there were not many clues or CCTV recordings. How did you nab them?' was the first question from a senior journalist.

'I will let Mr Anand Behari Rai, SP (city), brief you,' opined the senior officer.

Mr Rai leaned forward and, angling the microphone towards him, said, 'Well, it is a rather interesting story. This can be the screenplay for the next Bollywood film.' The three police officers looked at one another and smiled.

The gathered reporters politely smiled.

'During our on-site interrogation of witnesses, the bank cashier, Mr Rajendra Yadav, gave us a useful clue. While they were dragging the cash-laden trunks outside, Ravi Gupta's mobile phone buzzed. As he switched his attention to his cell phone, Mr Yadav made a valiant effort to overpower him. However, he was smashed on the face by this vermin here—but not before he had a chance to see the name flashing on the cell phone's screen. When we asked him if he was sure about the name, Mr Yadav replied that he could not miss it as the phone screen was as big as the PVR screen!' chuckled the superintendent.

The statement was met with loud laughter.

'We now had a name to work on. Mr Yadav remembered the name as Kuruswamy Kolkata on the phone screen. Hence, Mr Manoj Yadav and his team immediately got in touch with the cellular service providers at Kolkata. Kuruswamy, being an unusual name, it was not difficult to trace the number. It was a Reliance connection. Immediate search also revealed that a call had been made to an Allahabad circle number at 10.35 a.m. on Tuesday.

We traced this Airtel number to an Allahabad address in Katra. It was registered in the name of Ravi Gupta, and the telecom company's subscription application form's photograph also matched our records from the video feed.'

'But, sir, the CCTV had been compromised. You only told us,' interjected an alert reporter.

'Correct. But that is only half the story. Ashwani, the bank peon standing here'—he gestured to a dark, sallow-faced person—'had snatched the camera feed cable from the recording unit and plugged in a digital pen of old feeds into the recording AUX. But unknown to them, a single wide-angle camera is located in the desktop module kept at the operation manager's table, and its mini recording unit is hidden inside the CPU cover. From there onwards, it was a short walk to the rest of the accomplices.' Mr Rai sat back with a smile.

'Now, Mr Yadav of SOG, will fill in the blanks.'

'Thank you, sir. Indeed, it was a short walk. We cross-checked the call records of Ravi Gupta over the last six months. Intensive scrutiny was done for calls over the last ten days, and when these numbers were matrixed together, a pattern emerged. These numbers were put under electronic surveillance, and their locations constantly monitored. The rest was just swift police action.'

'Can you tell us, sir, how they managed to vanish in broad daylight?' queried a fresh reporter. Several heads nodded in assent.

The SSP leaned forward and spoke, 'During our interrogation session, they revealed just how they managed to vanish. As soon as they moved from the bank, they turned towards Kanpur Road crossing near high court. Then they continued on Kanpur Road for another one and a half kilometres till they reached Nehru Park. Since the park is now more or less defunct, it is being used as a parking lot for the huge vehicle transport trailers that you see of Maruti, Hyundai, etc. They had already negotiated with an empty covered trailer which was leaving for New Delhi that night. So within seven minutes of leaving from the bank, they had driven up the trailer ramp into the vast hold of the truck. Our roadblocks came into place just five minutes later.

They waited till late evening inside the truck, and then bidding goodbye to the truck driver, they departed for home. To allay suspicion if stopped for checking, they used a decrepit, old half-tonner army-auctioned vehicle filled with sand. The cash trunks were manually embedded into the sand and camouflaged. To avoid checking, they used the old Nehru Park–McMohan Lines road, which is a restricted area, and now in disuse.' The SSP sat back.

The police officer turned to the escorting detail and said, 'Take them away.'

As the criminals were pulled away, the SSP turned once again to the gathered reporters and said with a smile, 'And now, may I present the true heroes of this story? Please join me in welcoming Ms Urvashi Singh, branch head, and Mr Rajendra Yadav, cashier of Garuda Bank!'

The two bank officers entered, smiling and diffident to a standing applause.

Hukum Singh

Hukum Singh lay on his cot in the weak winter sun and contemplated his life—faded images from the past, mostly in olive green, passed before his eyes. Those few occasions when he was home on annual leave were just a blur. It really did not matter much to Hukum as his thirty-five years and nineteen days in the army had provided him with a never-ending cocktail of memories.

Upon his honourable discharge from the army, he was welcomed in his village as befitted a hero—after all, he had served the country for more than three decades with honour, except for a few drunken brawls and nightly sojourns behind his barracks for a few rounds of 'flash' during the Diwali season. A scorching, bellowed dressing-down by the regimental subedar major and a few well-placed batons by the military police had made those occasions unforgettable.

Hukum Singh turned on his side and adjusted the well-worn green beret under his head. After retirement, the morning hours hung heavy on him—evenings were kind to him and enjoyable in the company of his army-issue Mohun's XXX rum. It also fetched him the brotherhood of several villagers who thanked his army service and its liberal canteen rules.

His dozing was interrupted by light tugs near his head. He opened one eye to see his senior-most goat, Kabun Sahib, trying to tug his green beret from beneath his head. Kabun Sahib was christened after a Major Coburn, who happened to be Hukum Singh's first company commander. With due deference to Kabun Sahib's seniority, Hukum Singh gave him a half salute and eased his beret away. Any other goat would have been rewarded by an earthy collection of choicest abuses and a guided kick on its rump. Warmed by the winter sun, Hukum Singh closed his eyes and slept.

* * *

'There is an urgent telegram for Lance Naik Hukum Singh,' bellowed the mess subedar over the din in the sepoys' mess. Hukum Singh looked up from his thali with trepidation— telegrams rarely brought good news. He walked slowly towards the mess subedar, searching his face for some signs of the news. He suddenly ran as he spotted the glint of a smile behind the huge moustache of the subedar!

'Not so fast, Hukum Singh. First, promise laddus to everyone here,' said the subedar as he held the telegram aloft in his hands.

'A laddu for everyone,' panted Hukum.

'You have been blessed with a son. Both mother and child are well,' beamed Mess Subedar Harnam Singh and was instantly greeted with a mighty hug.

'And about time too! We thought that Hukum Singh will directly become a grandfather,' said Lance Naik Ramdhani Singh of B Company, First Battalion of the 1/7 Rajput. The mess reverberated with laughter.

Lance Naik Hukum Singh of Charlie Company, 1/7 Rajput, shot him a baleful look. The rivalry between Bravo Company and Charlie Company was legendary and was matched in vehemence only by the age-old rivalry of the Rajput Regiment with the Sikh and Gorkha regiments.

Hukum Singh's immediate happiness was marred by the sting of fathering a son after almost seven years of marriage. Sunehri Devi, whom he had married after courting for almost four years in the wheat and bajra fields of his native village, had to endure harsh comments from the family and village elders. Each homecoming of Hukum was looked upon as the arrival of the proverbial stork. At times, Hukum Singh felt as if he were being measured by the village womenfolk on his potency level. He wondered if there was a thermometer which he could put inside the old hags' backsides to determine their potency levels!

On several such occasions, seething with rage, Hukum Singh on annual leave, would swallow a few pegs of good old rum, and then swaying on his charpoy, he would announce in his parade ground voice, 'When I was screwing the Japanese in the Burma jungles, where were you, assholes? Do you know I killed more Japs with my dick than with my bayonet? Even today, they walk with their legs apart!'

In saner moments, he would curse God, the pathetic army leave structure, the mess cook, the company medic, and the women's ovulation cycle for his predicament. Once, after being treated for suspected syphilis with repeated shots of penicillin, he was convinced that the medical orderly had given him impotency shots to curb his ardour—with the active connivance of his subedar. For many nights, he could be seen near the med orderly room and JCO's mess with his "shaving razor to cut off their silly appendages!"

*   *   *

Pintoo, the three-year-old son of Yudhraj Singh and the first grandson of Hukum Singh, was watching the snoring, flaring nostrils of his grandfather with interest. It reminded him of the little monkey which sat on the roof and grated his teeth at all the neighbours. Descended from the brave Ahirs, Pintoo feared none. He put his index finger inside Hukum Singh's right nostril and peered closely as Hukum Singh's eyes and then cheeks twitched.

*   *   *

Hukum Singh was about to castrate the med orderly with his shaving razor when he felt the entry of a caterpillar inside his right nostril.

Shit!

It was trying to lay eggs on his septum!

Shit! Shit!

Hukum Singh sat bolt upright and glared at Pintoo. He shook his head to clear it of the castration images. Kabun

Sahib was still annoyed with him and turned his posterior to Hukum Singh's gaze.

Hukum looked at the sun and decided it was just past noon, time enough for a leisurely stroll in the field—and a smoke perhaps.

*　　*　　*

Hukum Singh was born in a well-to-do farmer's family in Dausa village, about fifty kilometres from Jaipur on the main Jaipur–Agra highway. The only male child between five sisters, Hukum Singh (or Paltu as he was popularly known) was thoroughly pampered and spoilt.

At a very early age, he had understood that he could get away with almost every mischief conceivable and made the most of it. To his doting parents and grandparents, Paltu was Rana Sanga and Kautilya all rolled into one.

From the age of six or seven years, Paltu had formed his own small band of followers, with whom he would spend hours playing soldier-spy. They had each sharpened a small stick and considered it to be their lance. They had seen British and Indian soldiers carrying their muskets and rifles with gleaming bayonets and spent many afternoons marching around the wheat and bajra fields with their sticks in a 'shoulder arms' position.

Paltu, as the leader, had tied a red rag on his lance and would charge up and down the temple stairs, shouting his war cry, '*Bol Bajrang Bali ki Jai.*' His jawans were supposed to answer with, '*Tharro todd denge Anda.*' (Loosely translated, it meant 'Will break your balls'). Now, the temple priest, a man of many virtues but with a short fuse, was unhappy with the day's earnings. It was a Tuesday, and he was expecting a collection of at least eight to twelve annas. The collection box held just about four annas and a few pice. His melancholy was broken by the shouted command of Paltu: *'Dasta, ageh badh!'* 'Squad, advance!'

The temple priest, Sant Gosain, a man of monumental proportions and with a ton of quivering flesh in his belly, stood up and decided to shoo away the raucous brigade. Suddenly he saw a small army of children rushing up the temple steps. Paltu screamed, *'Bol Bajrang Bali ki Jai,'* to be immediately answered by tiny danda-wielding sepoys, *'Tharro todd denge Anda.'* This was too much for Sant Gosain, and he lumbered up to the steps and shouted, *'Chal, tikree ho ja, nahin tha pachaso dande phutenge therre pichwado.'* Go, just vanish from here, or you will get fifty lathis on your backsides.

Paltu and his brave sepoys returned to the courtyard and gathered around the Hanuman Khambh. They looked again towards Sant Gosain, who was majestically standing on the top platform and was quivering his belly at them. To reinforce his words, he picked up a small mace, which was usually kept at the sanctum's entrance and shook it towards Paltu's army.

It is still not clear what happened—one moment, the chastised army was standing in the courtyard, and the other moment, they were charging up the steps led by Paltu's war cry. Sant Gosain's last memory was of shrill cries of *'Tharro todd denge Anda'* before baby bones met quivering flesh.

Paltu remembered stumbling on the last step and rocketing headlong into Sant's belly and his lance burying itself in the priest's groin. His other sepoys swarmed all over the swami, who lay like a beached whale clutching his midriff and trying to untangle Paltu's lance from his throbbing groin and dhoti folds. Paltu, obeying Newton's third law of motion, had ricocheted down the steps and now sat, catching his breath.

Scared by the funny wheezing sounds and the rolling eyes of the priest, the army retreated and dispersed silently to their homes.

That evening, the priest called a meeting of the village elders and secured a resolution barring the entry of small kids without parents on grounds of inadequate security. Some of the attending village elders were sorry to learn that Sant Gosain had developed arthritic pain in his groin and was finding it difficult to sit cross-legged. A slightly medically inclined villager noted with interest this case of abdominal arthritic pain. *Are there bones and joints in the stomach?* he mused, scratching the short hairs on his head.

Sant Gosain, using his executive powers, changed the temple's holy invocation to *'Pawan Putra Hanuman ki Jai.'* Any chant of *'Bol Bajrang Bali ki Jai'* found the swami clutching his groin in anticipated grief!

*   *   *

At the age of seventeen years, Hukum Singh joined the British Indian Army, and in the tradition of his forefathers, he joined the 1/7 Rajput. From the regulatory six months' basic training, it was cut short to four months of intensive back-breaking training schedule. The 1/7 Rajput had been designated to lead the Burma campaign.

From the scorching plains of Fatehgarh in United Provinces, the 1/7 Rajput was sent to the humid, dense forests of coastal Burma in the Arakan region. A two-week specialized jungle warfare training programme was launched, where, as per Hukum Singh, he learned to wage war against mosquitoes, pythons, and several varieties of cobra.

The First Battalion and Second Battalion of the 1/7 Rajputs were asked to advance into the Arakans via Dimapur. They were attached to the Fourteenth Indian Division and tasked with capturing the Mayu Peninsula and the Aykab Island, where an airfield of strategic importance was located. Its capture would seriously cripple the war efforts of the Imperial Japanese Army. At Imphal, the 1/7 Rajput along with 5/8 Punjab and First Battalion of the Royal Inniskilling Fusiliers were designated the Forty-Seventh Indian Infantry Brigade.

The roads and civil administration of eastern India were not geared for an army assault of this magnitude. The heavy Bedford trucks could not proceed beyond Imphal. From there on, the brigade had to walk through dense forests and mountain trails infested with leeches, pythons, and even alligators in the marshy swamplands.

The Forty-Seventh Indian Infantry Brigade finally met the Japanese in the dense mangrove forests just ten miles short of Donbaik.

*   *   *

For four days and nights, Sepoy Hukum Singh and others of C Company 1/7 Rajput, and E Company of the Royal Inniskilling Fusiliers had been wading through dense forests of bamboo and bracken, which clung and snapped at them. The soldiers had been issued with machetes as part of their jungle kit and used them to clear a path through the thick underbrush. The Royal Inniskilling Fusiliers were mainly Irish soldiers and were totally unprepared for this kind of jungle combat. Nothing had prepared them for this horror—hot, clammy weather; leeches and pythons on the muddy ground; deadly vipers and tree snakes hanging from branches as innocently as Christmas buntings; mosquitoes, by the thousands, with a vicious penchant for Irish blood; the cackling monkeys which seemed to be shadowing them and were not beyond snatching their water canteens or candy rations.

The Irish were on the verge of collective nervous breakdown!

*   *   *

Sepoy Hukum Singh and four other sepoys led by Jemadar Rann Singh were lying motionless in the mangrove forest for the last fifteen minutes or so. They were the point team, scouting ahead, and were now waiting for the main body to join up.

He felt a few bodies slithering past and tapped the one closest to him to lay still. He had heard a well-recognized sound.

Suddenly there was a pitter-patter of warm raindrops on his tin helmet and then the unmistakable smell of fresh urine. The realization dawned, and Hukum Singh rolled on to his back, aligned his Martini–Enfield .303 with the raindrops and fired.

'*Ped se muut rahe hain, Saale . . . Behenc—d*,' bellowed Hukum Singh. Sister fornicators are pissing from the trees.

A body in khaki with a jungle cap, clutching a rifle, fell near him. Never again would any Japanese soldier urinate from an elevation. After the war, it was made a part of the Japanese Imperial Army training manual!

By now, the Rajputs and the Irish were firing feverishly into the tall mangrove trees. The Japanese perched atop makeshift bamboo platforms were also sighting at the muzzle flashes below and firing. The Japanese, unable to change positions as they were wedged on to the platforms almost eighty feet up, were gradually getting decimated. The Rajputs and the Irish, terrified by the banshee wails of 'Banzai, Banzai, Banzai' coming from the trees along with bullets, spurred themselves like agile langurs to flit from tree to bush and bush to slush.

'*Maar saale Medhek madar c—d ko.*' Kill the motherfucking frog.

'*Bol Bajrang Bali ki Jai*,' yelled a sepoy, and it was answered with blood-curdling cries of 'Raja Ram Chandra ki Jai' as the Rajputs leaped up from their positions and charged, firing at the treetops.

Spurred by the charging Rajputs, the Royal Inniskilling Fusiliers also sprang up with their full-throated battle cry '*Faugh a Ballagh*' ('Clear the way'), firing at the hidden Japs above.

'*Abey, Suraj Mal . . . goli kyon nahi chalata hai re?*' yelled Jemadar Rann Singh at a trembling soldier who was trying to burrow deep into the soft earth. There was a subdued 'Aah . . .' and Jemadar Rann Singh turned to see blood gurgling out from Suraj Mal's throat.

The Japanese were now falling like autumn leaves, but still, shrill cries of 'Buta O koroshimasu' and 'Banzai' rent the air.

The smell of cordite and fear was nauseous, and Hukum Singh crawled underneath an imposing tree to change his magazine. He sighted along the barrel and squeezed the trigger. The body in the tree jerked but did not fall. Hukum Singh realized that the Jap was already riddled with bullets and dead.

The ground was covered with a forest of broken branches, leaves, and still bodies.

The few Jap survivors were now calling 'Jihi, Jihi' from the trees and waving their caps. A few were sitting with folded palms in abject supplication.

The Irish and the Rajputs got up cautiously and gestured to the Japanese to climb down. But first, they had to throw down their rifles and carbines.

The British Indian Army soldiers looked at the descending posteriors, and each one of them harboured a hidden desire to permanently fix his bayonet into the khaki bottoms. Sepoy Juggan Singh from Sikar could not hold himself and chased a weeping Jap with his bayonet. The Jap leaped up and threw a primed grenade at Juggan. The resulting explosion decimated both Sepoy Juggan Singh of Sikar and the Japanese warrior.

This skirmish was the only Japanese debacle in the Burma campaign of 1942. The British Indian Army could not ultimately dislodge the Japanese from their forward defence line around Rathedaung and Donbaik and were pushed back, leaving much of their heavy equipment behind.

Beaten, demoralized, exhausted, and riddled with cholera and dysentery, the British Indian Army retreated over 1,000 miles to Chittagong. History preserved them as the Forgotten Army.

*   *   *

Hukum Singh, Davedar Singh, and Mool Chand sat around the fire, with blankets warming their bodies and XXX rum warming their souls. Davedar Singh was a fellow ex-serviceman from the Brigade of Guards and, like Hukum Singh, spent most of his post-retirement hours gazing at the village belles, cattle, and dusty roads in this precise order. Mool Chand was recently retired from CRPF and, having carefully invested his retirement funds in bank monthly income schemes and some agricultural land, preferred to lace his evenings with free army-issue rum. For this, he had a small price to pay—tolerate the long yarns that Hukum Singh and Davedar Singh spun of their brave exploits in enemy land!

Davedar Singh tossed some small potatoes in the fire and asked Hukum Singh, 'Tell me, Hukum, what was the real reason for the Rajput–Gorkha war at Mhow?'

'*Arre, na yaar.* It was nothing. Just a small misunderstanding.'

'No, but I am told that you were awarded a Maha Vir Chakra for your actions that day,' Davedar persisted with a sly grin.

Mool Chand leaned forward and listened attentively. He knew when a good yarn was coming. Hukum Singh bent forward to shift a few potatoes in the fire and cleared his throat.

*　　*　　*

There was talk among the officers and ranks of 1/7 Rajput, that they would either be disbanded or merged with some other regiment. There was heavy resentment and dissent in the battalion because of this. The officers were trying to convince the ranks as well as themselves that there was no cause for any such action.

The 1/7 Rajput was a much-decorated battalion with one Param Vir Chakra, seven Maha Vir Chakra and more than fifty Vir Chakras. There had never been any issues with discipline or desertion; hence, such news was relegated to the back pages. However, one fine day, the commanding officer called for a battalion parade and broke the news that the First Battalion of the Rajput would be merged with the Brigade of Guards and would become the Fourth Guards Brigade. It is not easy for a battalion to sever its ties from its mother regiment, and First Rajput also succumbed to this melancholia. The officers, astutely judging the low morale and dissatisfaction of the troops, quickly drew up a plan to send the First Rajput on a two-month training course at the Infantry Combat School, Mhow.

On a cold winter day, some 840 officers and ranks boarded a military-special train from Amritsar bound for Indore, which was the nearest railhead to Mhow. The rake was made up of sleeper coaches as well as some covered wagons and flatcars to accommodate the men, essential supplies, and a few vehicles. The special siding at Amritsar railway station was a sea of olive-green uniforms, combat fatigues, black steel trunks with white-painted names, ranks, and serial numbers, SLRs, and bedding rolls. Slowly, the platform emptied, and with a rattle of creaking joints, couplers, and burdened track, the military-special train heaved. The platform vendors of puri sabzi, chai, and biscuits had done brisk business with the teeming soldiers, who now looked morosely at the departing train and commerce.

Each carriage was secured by a small detail of four soldiers, while the open flatcars with light vehicles carried a heavier sentry squad. Berths were quickly allotted to JCOs and NCOs, who set up their little empires with water canteens, winter parkas, small packets of biscuits, masala peanuts, and a copy of *Manohar Kahaniyan*, demarcating their area of actual control.

Military-special trains in times of war or national emergency are utmost-priority trains on the Indian Railways. In peacetime, these special trains are referred to as Faltoos and given track clearance only after all the train, vehicular, pedestrian, and animal traffic, including lost buffaloes, have crossed the lines. The standing joke was that the military-special trains were the ghost trains of Indian Railways, with no permanent abode or destination—nameless, faceless, sitting silently in desolate jungles and creepy marshalling yards.

Thus, this military-special train with the 1/7 Rajput chugged, stopped, loitered, and then chugged again crossing Jalandhar, Ludhiana, Ambala Cantt, New Delhi, and Hazrat Nizamuddin over forty-eight hours. It was clearing Mathura East Outer and passing by a level crossing when, with a squeal of brakes and lurching, grinding iron, it stopped. The train was halfway across the level crossing, and the poles were down, barring all vehicular traffic. The traffic kept building up on either side of the railway crossing, but the gates remained closed. The army men looked with little interest at the milling traffic around them. A group of schoolchildren got down from their school bus and came near the gates, looking with interest at the sea of green uniforms inside the carriages.

'*Bharat Mata ki jai*,' cried a tiny, shrill voice from the group of schoolchildren. There was pin-drop silence, and then a chorus of young voices repeated, '*Bharat Mata ki jai*.' The soldiers suddenly stiffened, and from inside the coach came harsh shouts of '*Bharat Mata ki jai*, jai, jai' with uniformed sleeves and fists punctuating the cry. The army men were now pressed closer to the windows and smiling at the children. There was a flurry of activity in other coaches also as more soldiers were peering out from the doors and windows of their bogeys.

The young schoolchildren, enthused with the response, gave a rousing shout of '*Bharat Mata ki Jai*'. Immediately hundreds of hard, proud soldiers from every carriage of the military-special train shouted, '*Bhaaaaraat Maata ki Jaaii, Jaaii, Jaaii*.' Each 'Jaaii' was accentuated by clenched fists, mirroring the resolve of these soldiers. By now, people on either side of the railway crossing had alighted from their vehicles and were thronging the tracksides to join in this spontaneous celebration. The railway yard master, signalman, and point switchman were also standing at the small landing on the track signal hut, watching this miracle unfold. The yard master's smile became a little broader when he saw the schoolchildren and others duck below the crossing poles and cross towards the army men.

The yard master turned and cranked his telephone. 'Mathura Central, East Outer . . . run caution on all sections as hundreds of people are here on the tracks at Roopgunj level crossing. No, no problems at all . . . Bharat Mata ki jai.'

The signal and traffic controller at Mathura Central junction about 800 metres down line was perplexed at the yard master's request. However, he dutifully clicked all incoming and outgoing traffic signals to amber to denote caution, running below fifteen kilometres per hour. The faint sounds of 'Bharat Mata ki jai' were now coming clearly from East Outer. He smiled and shook his head.

On the tracks, beaming soldiers and jubilant crowds stood face to face. The civilians again shouted, 'Bhaaaraat Maata kii Jaaii,' and the smiling soldiers thundered, 'Bol Bajrang Bali ki jai.' A sardarji, with his infant son perched on his shoulders, climbed upon a concrete slab and shouted, 'Jo bole so nihaal,' and the swelling crowds answered as one, 'Sat Sri Akal!'

Some of the soldiers had picked up the young schoolchildren in their arms and were trying to conjure up some biscuits and candy for them. Others were shaking hands and embracing the smiling, jostling crowds. On the houses and buildings adjacent to the tracks, the young and the old had all got out on their balconies and were waving and pointing. A few fruit sellers and vendors were trying their best to ply the smiling soldiers with their wares. Any attempt by the soldiers to pay was quickly denied with folded palms and a soft smile. 'Aap apne desh ki liye apni jaan de sakte hain, kya main aapko ek phal bhi nahi de sakta?' said a hunched-back Manohar Lal, who ran a cycle repair shop just near the crossing. A wizened old man in dirty pyjamas was trying to place a bunch of bananas into a soldier's hand and said, 'Main aapko kuch nahi de sakta . . . per ye qubool kariye.' The soldier just took his work-worn, shrivelled hand and kissed it.

The engine gave a long whistle and then two sharp blasts, a pause of thirty seconds, and then again the long blast. The smiling soldiers moved towards the train and climbed aboard. The train jerked and moved slowly. There were a thousand upturned fists and a thunderous cry of 'Bhaaaraat Maaata kiii jaaiii'. The soldiers replied, their voices husky with emotion, 'Bol Bajrang bali ki jai' and 'Raja Ram Chandra ki Jai'. The civilians on the tracks, the schoolchildren in their uniforms, and the departing soldiers all were waving and trying to crystallize this scene in their eyes forever. The yard master wiped a tear from his eyes and gestured to the gateman and signalman to release the poles.

Many of the schoolchildren, on reaching home, told their parents about this wonderful event and announced their intentions of joining the Indian Army. Many of the soldiers were so exhilarated by this public display of love, respect, and admiration that they forsook their evening meal and said, 'Pet to aaj khushiyon se hi bhar gaya!'

*　　*　　*

The military-special train slowly meandered its way across the Great Indian Plain and the Chambal ravines through Gwalior and Guna, lying in wait on loop lines for high-priority trains to pass by, at times being allocated the Gadha line, which was used to shunt engines, bogeys, and railway detritus. A diversion to any Gadha line meant a wait of more than four hours, and the soldiers had learned to employ these hours in washing clothes and cleaning utensils. Some of the havildars also employed these stops to fall in their companies and have impromptu drills and exercises.

At one such stop, C Company of Havildar Hukum Singh went on a run through the neighbouring fields of half-ripened wheat. The company chanted its doggerel in the same cadence as it ran:

> Chand ke upar chadd baitha hoon,
> Neend na aaye, jag raha hoon,
> Apni jholi bech raha hoon,
> Juniors ke main le raha hoon,
> Ek Do Teen Char
> Ustad bada hoshiar.

The village womenfolk, unused to seeing hulking men in combat fatigues with rifles slung across their shoulders, raised a cry and fled for home, pulling their children along.

Cries of 'Daku, Daku, Bhaag, Daku Aaya' galvanized the others.

Soon, heads were popping up from all the neighbouring fields and then shooting across the mud paths towards their village. The scarecrows, savouring the winter sun, cackled with glee at this human exodus and merrily flapped their raggedy limbs. This was certainly better than scaring crows, mynahs, and herons!

After five nights and six days of travel, the military-special train reached Indore just as twilight set in.

*   *   *

The infantry combat school at Mhow was inaugurated on 1 January 1948 for the express purpose of training the infantry, correctly termed as the most potent combat wing. Spread over a thousand acres, it had all kinds of geophysical terrains, training equipment, and weapons. Most importantly, the instructors here were the best that the army had to offer.

All infantry warfare doctrines are tried, tested, improved, and preserved here. More than 10,000 infantry soldiers undergo training every year in all aspects of weapon handling, firing, camouflage, unarmed combat, battalion support weaponry, radio communication, etc. The Army Markmanship Unit (AMU) is also quartered here.

The 1/7 Rajput was billeted in the Thimayya barracks, just off the CSD canteen, and adjacent to the open amphitheatre. A short distance away, in the Veer barracks were men of the 1/11 Gorkhas, almost on the verge of finishing their eight-week course and rejoining their unit in Pathankot.

The mornings were full of cross-country runs, physical training, and the field classes immediately after breakfast. The technical and theory classes were scheduled for the afternoons to be followed by tea, games, and evening entertainment.

Early one morning, the Rajputs and Gorkhas happened to meet near the Udhi heavy weapons firing range on their morning run. This firing range was about seven kilometres from their barracks. The two squads fell in step and kept running.

Suddenly Lance Naik Jasveer Singh of the Rajputs stepped up the pace and started chanting 'Ek Do Teen Char . . . Ustad Bada Hoshiar.' The Gorkhas, not to be outdone, increased their pace and, while passing the Rajputs, chanted, '*Nitambho pe dulatta, hariyo nasta.*' A kick on your ass will be your healthy breakfast!

The Rajput troops, with their height advantage and longer strides, easily caught up with the jogging Gorkhas and pulled ahead. As the Rajputs could not understand the wicked chant of the Gorkhas in Nepalese, they continued to sing 'Ek Do Teen Char . . .'

Sepoy Nar Bahadur Tamang could not tolerate the jeering of the passing Rajputs and called out to Havildar Jung Bahadur, '*Hamilai yi Bewakoofon dekhaun garaun.*' Let us show these idiots.

Havildar Jung Bahadur, in keeping with the tradition of his martial clan, sprinted ahead and swerved in front of the Rajputs, and grabbing his ass cheeks with both hands behind his back, he spread them and shouted, '*Thulo khate Gadha-haru.*' Big-assed donkeys.

The Gorkhas, happy as monkeys, sprinted after Havildar Jung Bahadur, gladly spread their ass cheeks in front of the hypnotized Rajputs, and shouted, '*Thulo khate Gadha-haru.*' A few Gorkhas, with their digestive juices flowing after this morning run, reinforced the insult with smelly, voluminous, and crackling farts.

The Rajputs stung by the insolence of the Gorkhas gave chase, hurling abuses. Havildar Hukum Singh shouted, 'Rank todd aur daur.' Break ranks and run.

The Rajputs broke rank and sprinted, shouting, 'Saale, Natwe.' Bloody dwarfs. Within a few seconds, the Gorkhas also broke ranks and sprinted. It was difficult to determine between the hunter and the hunted. For those fortunate enough to see this spectacle, it would remain with them forever—the sight of six-foot-plus Rajputs with flowing moustaches running for their lives alongside five-foot-nothing Gorkhas with hardly a whisker on their faces. The early morning campus traffic of supply and mess trucks, a few more exercising squads, and officers on morning walk all pulled aside to let this human juggernaut pass.

The distance of seven kilometres was covered in a matter of twenty-one minutes, which was normally completed in twenty-five to twenty-six minutes. Sepoys Nar Bahadur Rai and Harihar Singh were neck to neck over the last fifty metres, snorting and panting like mountain mules in heat. Nar Bahadur clenched his teeth and put every last ounce of strength in his legs to carry him through; Harihar Singh lowered his head and leaned forward to increase his stride. He was the 800- metre-run battalion champion. From the corner of his eyes, Rai saw Harihar Singh inching ahead. Defeat is unacceptable to any Gorkha, and Nar Bahadur Rai was no exception. He swerved slightly to the right and, with his right foot, lightly tapped on the left ankle of Harihar

Singh, who took wings and literally flew through the last ten feet to land in a heap near the parade ground mike. He cleared the line first.

Nar Bahadur also completed his last few feet in flight mode, propelled by a kick on his behind by a burly Rajput who had seen him tripping Harihar Singh. The huffing, puffing, wheezing soldiers crossed the line and collapsed. Bruised ankles, bums, and egos were the major casualties of the day.

'Katars and kukris were the visual signals exchanged between the Rajputs and the Gorkhas!

* * *

The Rajputs and the Gorkhas are both formidable fighters, with a long history and tradition of martial skills. Stories of Rajput valour abound over the last several hundred years—from Prithviraj Chauhan, Rani Padmini of Chittor, Rana Sanga, Maharana Pratap, Hadi Rani to the present-day brave hearts like Jadu Nath Singh. Honour, victory, chivalry, and fearlessness are all indelible traits of Rajputs.

Gorkhas, similarly, are honour-bound, fearless, brave to the point of insanity, and relentless in their pursuit of victory. They are rightly referred to as the world's most ferocious fighters, and even Rommel's famed Afrika Korps were afraid of these Gorkha soldiers. It is said that late into the nights, Gorkha soldiers, with their kukris held in their hands, would slither across the sands at El Alamein, inside German infantry positions, and behead all those unfortunate enough to lie in their path! And then, just as silently, they would melt into the darkness and British forward lines. The sight of a Gorkha charging with his unsheathed kukri is an unforgettable seismic event!

Defeat is unacceptable and unknown to both.

Interestingly, Gorkhas and Rajputs love to dance and sing. And they both have a particularly typical way of dancing—by bending from the waist to one side, with the reciprocal hand raised at an angle and their heads also tilted to one side!

*   *   *

The Rajputs were marching back to the mess at lunchtime after a gruelling session of unarmed combat training when they came upon the Gorkhas practising Dhaawa at the Albert Ekka combat ground. Not to miss a chance of witnessing Gorkha hand-to-hand combat, Subedar Rann Singh called a halt and ordered the troops to be at ease. Some of the Rajputs squatted under the camouflage nettings, while the others stood.

The Gorkhas, in full battle gear, with black-streaked faces, twigs on their helmet webbing, and rifles with bayonets in place, were stepping up in lines of six. The instructors were standing at the base mark and at the stuffed targets located thirty yards away, watching every move of the Gorkhas.

Havildar Nar Bahadur Gurung hissed, 'Taiyaar [*ready*],' and then a thundering bellow, 'Dhaawwwwaaaaa [*charge*]'.

From pint-sized soldiers, the Gorkhas transformed into demonic apparitions. They stomped their left feet forward, crouched, and then with a mixture of sprint, leaps, and bounds, they covered the first twenty yards, emitting strange, unintelligible cries. Then the skies were rent with the chilling battle cry of the Gorkhas: 'Jai Mahakali. Ayo Gorkhali.' Victory to Mahakali. Here come the Gorkhas!

Crouching, stomping, with their bayonets extended like rigid lances, the Gorkhas swerved, feinted, deflected, and pierced the stuffed dummies with blood-curdling yells. 'Do Anni Anni,' shouted the havildar, and the Gorkhas again plunged their bayonets with furious power into the targets. Having completed their task, they stomped ten paces away before breaking rank.

The second line came up. The same commands and furious engagement followed, except that on the second plunging, Jawan Ganga Bahadur Limbu could not withdraw his bayonet in the prescribed motion—the point had probably become ensnarled in the innards of the dummy. Embarrassed, Ganga Bahadur pulled his bayonet out with all his might. The result was what mess stories are made of. Ganga Bahadur not only pulled his bayonet out but managed to unseat the dummy, which toppled on top of Ganga Bahadur. Ganga Bahadur was pinned underneath with his booted legs around the torso of the dummy in the classic sexual missionary position.

'Put it deeper, put it harder,' cried Shiv Singh of the Rajputs, grinding his pelvis. A howl of laughter went up from the watching Rajputs at the sexual assault on Ganga Bahadur. The jawan disentangled himself from the embrace of the dummy, and with a flaming-red face completed the last ten steps.

Ganga Bahadur, suffused with impotent rage and embarrassment, stepped towards the distant Rajputs and, with his rifle cradled across his chest, let out a frenzied cry. His face and limbs were jerking and quivering as if he had been electrocuted. The other Gorkhas were also standing tensed.

A cold, hard stare from the senior instructor was correctly interpreted by Subedar Rann Singh, who ordered his squad to fall in and marched them off.

*   *   *

Two days prior to their departure, on a cold December evening, the Gorkhas gathered around near the amphitheatre and started a small bonfire. The Subedar Major Bhumi Bhan Gurung raised a toast and yelled, 'Jai Gorkhali.' There were immediate cries of 'Jai Gorkha' by the assembled jawans.

These were men of the 1/11 Gorkhas, with the Batalik battle honours to their name for their exemplary bravery in capturing Tololing Peak during the Kargil war. This battalion was composed mostly of Rais and Limbus from the eastern regions of Nepal. As an eye witness account of the final battle of Tololing did the rounds and went viral over the Internet, the Gorkhas attained eternal fame:

> The 1/11 Gorkhas were tasked with clearing the Khalubar post on Tololing. The Pakistanis were well entrenched atop Khalubar and had fortified bunkers to

protect them from the elements as well as armed attacks and shelling. The Gorkhas, numbering about thirty-five and led by Lieutenant Colonel Lalit Rai, started the climb. Each step was fraught with danger as the ascending slope was fully exposed to the Pakistani post, which had a clear field of fire on the advancing Indian troops. Losing many men, the Gorkhas continued to advance.

After a bloody hand-to-hand combat for capturing the eight Pakistani bunkers at Khalubar Peak, in which the Gorkhas wielded their kukris with deadly effect, chopping off Pakistani heads, the Gorkhas finally killed them all. The Pakistanis occupying other peaks and positions were watching the heads roll down the slopes. Finally, only eight Gorkhas were left under the command of Lieutenant Colonel Rai to defend this newly captured peak. This peak was vital to the Pakistanis as it overlooked their supplies route as well as some other Pakistan-occupied features. It was imperative for the Pakistanis to regain it. By nightfall, they had assembled a company-size attack unit of about 115–120 soldiers, who commenced their climb. As soon as they were within firing range, the Gorkhas made them retreat with a hail of withering fire. The Pakistanis retreated with heavy casualties. They again regrouped and attacked, twice, and each time, they were driven back by the well-directed fire of the entrenched Gorkhas. By now, the Gorkhas were almost out of ammunition.

The decimated Pakistani force, now numbering only thirty-five to forty, pushed forward for a final assault. As the Gorkhas were almost zero on ammunition, they let the Pakistanis approach. As they drew nearer, the Pakistanis targeted the Indian commanding officer with choicest abuses in Punjabi. Lieutenant Colonel Rai replied as best as he could, and then to break the steel-taut tension in the eight surviving Gorkhas, he said, 'These Pakistani louts are abusing your commanding officer, and you all are sitting still?' The Gorkhas looked at one another. It is very rare for a Gorkha soldier to abuse—he believes more in the power of his arms and kukri. However, they had to shield their CO from the abusive offense. Finally, Gyan Bahadur shouted from behind a rock, '*Pakistani Kutta, Tum idhar aayega to hum tumhara mundi kat dega.*' Pakistani dogs, if you come this way, then we will behead you all.

Colonel Rai, to ease the tension, said, 'The Pakistanis will surely die today, but they will die laughing at Gyan Bahadur's abusive prowess.' The Gorkhas laughed the laugh of the mad and the condemned—they had now nothing to lose but their lives!

The Gorkhas took out their beloved kukris and started sharpening them on the surrounding rocks and boulders. They started chanting, *'Abo tah kukri nikalera taeslai thik paarchhu.'* We will take out our kukris now and set them right.

The Pakistanis, now hardly fifty yards away, recoiled in fear, hearing the clang of the sharpening kukris and the ringing maddening laugh of the Gorkhas—they had not forgotten the rolling chopped-off heads of their unlucky comrades. The surviving Gorkha officer Lieutenant Colonel Rai and the eight surviving Gorkhas, in an act of bravery unparalleled to this day in any army, asked for artillery fire on themselves—their logic, if they have to die, then they must take the maximum number of enemies with them!

The Indian artillery officer manning the forward observation post many miles away was flummoxed at this request but, heeding the request of the determined Gorkhas, commenced firing using the Indian Gorkha positions as his reference point. The heavy Bofors gun fired.

The advancing Pakistanis, now hardly twenty to thirty yards away, were being blown to smithereens as the Indian shells exploded among them. The Gorkhas now leaped from their positions with their unsheathed kukris and the deadly war cry, 'Jai Mahakaali, Ayo Gorkhali.' The enemy soldiers, choosing between certain death and retreat, chose to retreat. On their way down, they were ambushed by the 1/11 Gorkha reinforcements climbing up, and they simply surrendered!

*   *   *

The Gorkhas sat around the bonfire and swilled their rum rations in their tin mugs—these tin mugs had been companions of soldiers worldwide for more than a century—and recounted the day's happenings. Some looked at the swilling rum with greed, others with pure, unadulterated love, and a few gazed solemnly into the bottom with gloomy eyes!

Shiv Dutt Rai was considered to be a good singer, and his singing improved with every peg. By the end of any concert, Shiv Dutt had to be carried off the stage with his lyrics and tunes also in inebriated disarray. Today, he sat looking morosely into his mug and was trying to solve a serious mathematical problem. He had received a letter today from his wife in Nepal that she was three months pregnant. Shiv Dutt had returned to the unit in August from annual leave, which was four months back. Now, how was she three months into pregnancy? Thirty days hath September, April,

June, and November . . . The mental maths became too much for Shiv Dutt, and he let go of the sorrowful thread. Rum, in any case, is a much-loyal bed fellow!

A few Gorkhas who saw Shiv Dutt staring into his tin mug started to softly beat a tattoo on their upturned mug bottoms. It would surely revive Shiv Dutt, they assumed. Shiv Dutt looked up and, with tears threatening to roll, softly sang the first few bars of '*Tapaile malai dukh deeno bh, raati ko neend khosera*'. You have given me sorrow and robbed me of my sleep. The Gorkhas quietened down and listened. Very soon, quite a few of them were adding their salty tears to the army rum.

A hundred yards away, in the Cariappa barracks, the Rajputs listened to the sentimental singing of the Gorkhas, which by now had become a concerto of rarefied sobbing and weeping. Some cried for their lost loves, some for their unfaithful wives, while the majority looked and wept at their subedar major, Jung Bahadur Limbu!

Hukum Singh, sitting on his charpoy, was polishing his boots. Next to him, Neta Ram was lying on his cot and trying to write a love letter to his wife of seven years. On any of his brighter days, it took him the better part of three hours to frame a three-paragraph letter. Today, with the Gorkhas wailing in the background, he was unable to string a few sentences also (not that his wife could make out, anyways)!

Hukum Singh looked at Neta Ram and said, 'Here, you polish my boots, and I will write your love letter to your wife.'

'I will break all your bloody teeth and stuff it down your throat.'

Hukum Singh ran his lips over his slightly protruding teeth and took a backseat. He looked fine this way, thank you!

Neta Ram tried to write for a few more minutes and then gave up. He sat up and shouted, 'Shut up, idiots.'

An enterprising sepoy, Kundan Singh, went out and, cupping his mouth, shouted, 'Shut up, shut up! Neta Ram is trying to write a love letter.'

A few catcalls and howls followed him back. A richly polished boot borrowed from Hukum Singh landed on his face as he came inside. An enraged Neta Ram confronted him, 'Are you from my *paltan* or theirs?'

'Your writing and their singing are in the same league. Hence, *you* must be from *that* paltan,' countered Kundan Singh.

'Shut up, you oafs.'

By now, the Gorkhas were at their soprano best, singing in almost a shrill shriek.

'Shut up, you bunch of *churails*,' shouted a voice from the Rajput barracks. In Indian folklore, a churail is a female ghost with a nasal voice and with feet that has toes at the back and heels in front.

In reply, the shrieks became a little louder, and the melody properly skewed.

Havildars Hukum Singh, Paan Singh, Kundan Singh, Neta Ram, Vijay Rathore, Fateh Bahadur, and Ram Surat Singh came out of the barracks and shouted, 'Shut up, you ghouls, or we will put our dicks up your sorry throats.'

The din subsided, and a drunken Nepali called, 'Your dicks are already up your royal arses, bloody *muchhars*!' There was a huge howl of laughter from the singing churails.

Now, to a Rajput warrior, his moustache is a sign of his valour and honour. Any disrespect to it can invite war. And invite war it did.

The seven Rajputs ran towards the merry-making Gorkhas and pounced upon them. Each burly Rajput was trying to strangle two Gorkhas simultaneously, and each Gorkha was trying to rip off the moustaches of two Rajputs simultaneously.

Shiv Dutt, the singing minstrel, was parked around the waist of Kundan Singh, and, with both hands, was trying to pull off Kundan Singh's six inches of curly moustache. Kundan Singh, on his part, was careening around the ground with Shiv Dutt wrapped around him and was trying to bang him into as many people, pillars, and objects as possible. Their careening and screeching kept the mosquitoes away.

Hukum Singh and the others were busy trying to fend off the horde of Gorkhas jumping on them from every angle. Most of the Gorkhas were trying to levitate the Rajputs by pulling their whiskers. A few were trying to find the eyes with their fingers, and a few more, in alcohol-induced stupor, were pirouetting around on their toes, trying to land a ball-breaker kick to the Rajput loins!

The mini war brought more of the paltan running from their barracks. It was now a full-scale war with fists, kicks, bamboo mosquito poles, and helmets being the preferred weapons of destruction. Rajput Might met Gorkha Guile, and both came out battered, bruised, but not evidently saner!

In the thick of battle arrived the regimental military police to restore order. Blowing their whistles and using their batons, the MPs waded in. They used their batons with wild abandon and treated the warring soldiers of both regiments with equal disdain. Hukum Singh was sitting on top of Padam Kumar Rai and was trying to decorate his face with left and right punches. Padam Kumar Rai, in turn, was trying to wrench off the starched moustache of Hukum Singh. A burly MP intervened and, catching Hukum Singh by the throat, tried to pull him backwards.

Hukum Singh let go of Padam Rai and turned his full fury on the MP. He lowered his head and charged directly into the torso of the MP, taking him backwards and downwards with his momentum. Padam Rai, not to be left behind, joined Hukum Singh in punishing the errant MP. While Hukum was trying to lock the MP in a half nelson, Padam was busy trying to unlock the handcuffs chained to the MP's belt. Unable to open the same, he decided to open the uniform trousers of the MP instead and set about unbuttoning his fly.

By now, the Gorkhas and Rajputs were fighting the MPs together, and most of the MPs could be seen retreating with whistles, torn shirts, and lanyards and armbands askew. Two more truckloads of military police arrived to reinforce their hammered brethren.

Cries of 'Ayo Gorkhali' and 'Bol Bajrang Bali ki Jai' rent the air as the Rajputs and Gorkhas enthusiastically prepared for another round with the MPs. The military police now formed a skirmish line and kept a respectful distance. Fortunately, the JCOs of both battalions arrived and (with a few well-chosen expletives) ordered their men to fall back and disperse. The men limped back to their respective barracks.

*   *   *

Sunday morning, and the Gorkhas were departing. A long line of three-tonners waited by the dispersal area. The luggage and weapons had already been loaded. The final round of last-minute shipments was also done, and the soldiers were now standing in company formation.

Subedar Major Bhumi Bahadur Gurung brought the parade to attention and then a sharp command to break ranks and board. The soldiers took three paces forward and then broke right. They started jogging towards the standing trucks, which had their engines running. As they clambered aboard, they heard a baritone voice singing:

> *Basa hai Aama, Gayou hai Baba,*
> *Lap bhey aan ke deena, mur ke au laut na*
> *deena.*

It is one of the most-loved and poignant folk songs of the Gorkhas, depicting the assurances of a departing soldier to his parents that he will definitely see them if he returns alive.

They saw a lone Rajput soldier in full ceremonial uniform standing near the landscaped hillock. Suddenly a few hundred soldiers of 1/7 Rajput converged from behind the hillock and, with a full-throated roar, sang:

> *Basa hai Aama, Gayou hai Baba,*
> *Lap bhey aan ke deena, mur ke au laut na*
> *deena.*

Those Gorkhas who had boarded stepped down and joined the others with lumps in their throats. And then softly they carried the song forward. The two battalions, bound by the tenets of honour, dignity, and valour from times immemorial, were, after all, brothers in arms.

The Gorkhas saluted to the Rajputs and, waving, climbed aboard. The Rajputs also stepped forward, and Havildar Hukum Singh, ramrod straight, commanded, 'Battalion, salute!' Almost eight hundred arms rose as one in a fitting tribute from one brave battalion to another.

Eyes misted with tears, and breaths became sighs on both sides as the Gorkhas departed, singing, 'Basa hai Aama . . .'

*   *   *

The wheat was about to be harvested, and marriages finalized. This was a good crop, and the farmers were envisaging a decent cash inflow. There were laughter and impromptu singing in the households as the women got busy preparing for crop harvest, threshing, and transport.

Hukum Singh, enjoying the evident happiness of his family, friends, and neighbours, could be seen walking around the crop-rich fields with a lathi every night to keep the hedgehogs and marauding troops of nilgais away. The scarecrows, now almost hidden by the towering golden wheat corns, always kept an eye out for Hukum Singh and happily flapped their arms and rolled their heads at his arrival.

For a soldier never dies . . .

The Nawab of Bilaul

'Pass me some fresh paan, not the sorry-looking leaves you gave me this morning,' spouted Mian Muazzam Ali, the current nawab of Bilaul, as he lay spread-eagled on the knotted charpoy. A few red drops of betel juice went up in the air and quickly descended on his face.

Nathu, the village *hajjam* (barber), quickened his ministrations of rubbing mustard oil on the nawab's legs. The soft voice of nawab saheb was a decoy. His volcanic vocal eruptions, complete with ornamental abuses, red betel nut lava, and spittle, could only be a sentence away! Nathu had no intentions of being fossilized in the nawab's spittle for his grandchildren to wonder at this man-made Pompeii and discreetly brought his *gamchha* (towel) to cover his head and face.

Mehangoo, the nawab's personal servant, quickly pushed two small cubes of betel leaves laced with nuts, lime, and peppermint into the gaping hole of the nawab's mouth.

Mian M. Ali choked and sat up in a single motion. '*Bewakoof* [idiot], you think my mouth is the kitchen furnace where you are stuffing bloody coal?' The nawab was prone to his own amalgam of English when things became too exciting for him. He straightened himself and swung his right arm to cuff Mehangoo behind the ears. Mehangoo, a veteran of many such attacks, neatly ducked under the arc of the nawab's arm. Nathu, with his peripheral vision blocked by his towel, received a tight cuff on the back of his head, which sent his volcanic shield flying across the courtyard.

Mehangoo laid himself prone on the cobbled floor of the courtyard and cried, '*Huzoor*, forgive me, forgive me.' Nathu, with a stinging medulla oblangata, was trying to count the stars as they happily danced in front of his eyes.

The nawab, in all his oily semi-naked glory, strode towards the *gosalkhana* (bathing room).

*   *   *

Mian Muazzam Ali was the eleventh generation of nawabs to rule Bilaul. Bilaul was a small principality in the United Provinces (earlier Oudh) and lay between Sultanpur and Faizabad. The estate had been granted to the ancestors of the present nawab by His Majesty Aurangzeb, the last of the Great Moguls.

Bilaul and its neighbouring countryside were a fertile region with two harvests of rabi and kharif crops as well as a small window for cash crops. In some parts, sugarcane was a major revenue earner, and in the recent past, quite a few *khansari* (sugar mill) units had come up.

This year, the crops were good, as were the monsoons. The previous three years (1933–35) had been terrible, and the eastern region was beset with very poor crops, resulting in a massive famine and cholera epidemic. To make matters worse, two years ago, Bihar and the adjoining areas were devastated by an earthquake of gigantic proportions.

Mian Muazzam Ali, the eleventh nawab of Bilaul, was the erring husband to two begums, father to nine legitimate children of assorted ages and at least three illegitimate children, and at his current age of fifty-six, was still raring to sow his wayward seeds. He was also the proud owner of a set of dentures (imported from England), an open-top Hudson car, a pair of Alsatians, two thoroughbred horses—Rana and Shiva—as well as a retinue of thirty-nine household staff, including munshis, *khadim*s, and jamadars.

Nawab saheb was of fragile build, with fine bones and chiselled features. His milk-white complexion was further enhanced as he had almost no hair on his body, except for a few strands of longish white hair on his cheeks which he insisted on categorizing as his *nawabi* beard. However, God had been kind on his crowning glory—he had a full head of silvery grey hair falling over his ears and curling at the nape of his neck. His begums, aware of his vanity, referred to him in moments of marital endearment as *mere huzoor-e guldusta* (my flowery lord)!

The nawab stretched his legs in the porcelain bathtub as his khadims soaped his body with Clifton lavender body soap (made in England) and poured warm water over him. Before the soap, he had been scrubbed with *besan* (gram flour) to remove the oil and to dislodge any particles of dirt. No less than three khadims were so productively employed, while another three stood behind the wooden partition with towels, talcum powder, and his freshly starched clothes.

Mian M. closed his eyes and imagined Billoo, the voluptuous maid-in-waiting to his senior begum, pouring scented water over him and caressing the soap suds away from his chest. He tingled with wanton lust and squeezed his thighs together. However, his member, disregarding the nawab's attempt at propriety, sprang up in salute, and the purple tip floated over the soapy suds. Mujibur, the youngest of his khadims, cupped the soapy foam and poured it over the nawabi knob in an effort to hide it from the others.

After forty-five minutes of wallowing in the bathtub, Mian M. stood up like a spiky monolith and, with the help of his khadims, navigated his way to the waiting servants to be dressed.

Having been towelled dry, the nawab was doused with a full can of St Ludwig's perfumed talcum powder and half a bottle of his favourite eau de cologne. The nawab was to be particularly embellished today as his friend from college, Zamindar Biltoo Khan, would be reaching this evening for a week-long stay.

Mian M. squinted with glee as he remembered the happy days spent at Colvin Taluqdars' College, learning Latin, maths, and science. To Mian M. and his close circle of friends, every subject seemed as incomprehensible as Latin, and Latin seemed to be from another world! *Estapor Medna Culpa* or some crazy phrases like this made up the total Latin imbibed by the future rulers of British India.

*   *   *

Nawab saheb and his friend Zamindar Biltoo Khan sat on golden-threaded sheets, surrounded by bolsters of several sizes. A silver hookah was placed between them, and the two friends kept passing the rubber pipe to each other after every few puffs. The hookah gurgled in appreciation at the delicate *tehzeeb* (grace) of the two hookah smokers—after all, only the aristocracy cupped and gurgled with such sublime finesse!

Zamindar Biltoo Khan was quite a character and much loved by all for his carefree, raucous, and bawdy ways. He was just about five feet tall, with pigeon legs and pigeon chest, sparkling eyes, bones as fragile as bone china, and a hooked nose with streaming white hair protruding from both his nostrils. Despite his size and structure, Biltoo Khan always walked with a swagger that could put any famed wrestler to shame. And with alcohol inside him, he was a single stick of dynamite with a short fuse. A consummate lover of Bacchus, Biltoo Khan rarely ever reached his bed on his own two legs.

His friends always recounted with glee Biltoo Khan's first (and last) encounter with his father-in-law, Vilayat Khan, right after his nikah. Brimming with happiness and loaded with imported wine on the grand occasion of his marriage, Biltoo Khan was escorted into the *shamiana*, where the bride's father, uncles, and brothers were waiting to welcome him and share the celebratory lunch with them. As soon as Biltoo Khan saw his father-in-law, all six feet three inches of him in coal-black skin with a patch over his left eye, in his drunken state, he exclaimed, 'Lahoul vila kuvat, yeh kaun bashar hai? Sub shakl-e-langur, fakad, dum ki kasar hai.' Loosely translated, it meant, 'By the might of

Allah, who is this creature with the face of a monkey? And only the tail is missing!'

Biltoo Khan's father-in-law had to be physically restrained from strangling his new son-in-law. Biltoo Khan was banned from visiting his in-laws, and it was said that Vilayat Khan kept a framed photograph of Biltoo in his almirah and, every morning after prayers, would religiously whack it with his leather chappals.

The nawab of Bilaul, Mian Muazzam Ali, was a similar bantam. Once, when the British deputy commissioner was invited for dinner, the nawab sat with him on the golden mattresses. As a special gesture in honour of the British official, he gestured for the dancing girls to begin. The commissioner, not wanting to offend the nawab, suffered the gyrations of the nautch girls with polite interest. Wine, fruits, nuts, and assorted meats cooked over slow fire were offered to the guests. Nawab saheb offered his silver hookah to the commissioner, who declined politely.

Mehangoo, the personal servant, had filled the hookah with the nawab's favoured tobacco, and in keeping with the evening's importance, he had also added a dash of opium to the bowl. For some reason, Mian M., riding high on the effects of opium, felt that the British officer was eyeing one of the nautch girls with obvious interest and, tapping him on his arm, said, 'If you want, I can arrange for the pink one to share the bed with you tonight. Oh, look at her two lovely ripe mangoes, just like our ripened *dussehri*s!'

'Nawab saheb, I think you have had one too many and are not in your senses. I should go now. Bearer, *gadi lagwao*,' the officer said, getting up.

'Where are you going, my sweet sir? Sweet as my lollipop,' crooned Mian Muazzam as he tried to pull the British officer back on to the mattress.

'Let go of my hand, you bloody idiot.'

'Idiot, you call me idiot? You bloody rascal *firangi*! Bloody red langur! Bloody camel dung. I will whip your ass just now.' And so shouting, an inebriated, intoxicated Mian M. jerked the hose from the hookah and slashed at the British officer. When Mian M. slashed a second time, the officer caught the hose and jerked it forward. Mian M., holding on to the other end, was now sprawled at the feet of the deputy commissioner. In one gallant sweep of his hand behind the officer's knee, Mian M. brought him crashing down.

The British officer, now hyperventilating with rage, smashed a solid punch to the nawab's face. 'Bloody motherfucker, I will break your neck' was his hissed threat.

'You bloody son of a whore, descendant of a fucking bare-assed mongoose! Bloody red-faced langur. Bloody rubbish! Bloody, smelly rectum of a *churail*!'

By now, the munshis and the other *khidmatgaar*s had pulled nawab saheb into a sitting position and were hastily escorting the burra sahib out. Nawab Mian Muazzam Ali was thereafter safely laid on his bed with an ice pack on his swollen nose.

The next morning, Mian Muazzam Ali awoke to a swollen nose and urgent summons to the British governor's residence in Lucknow.

He returned after a week, chastised and poorer by Rs.25,000/-, being the cost of damages levied on him. The British *laat* saheb had taken a lenient view and not put him in prison because of the services rendered to the Crown by the nawab's forefathers. The laat saheb, in private, had thoroughly enjoyed the narrative of the incident and secretly relished the comeuppance served to Mr Havell, the deputy commissioner.

However, Nawab Mian Muazzam Ali unwittingly had become a hero and, with every telling over the gurgling hookah, decorated the narrative with a fresh infusion of imaginary whiplashes and abuses. Those present on these unforgettable occasions were all praise for the nawab's extensive repertoire of abuses and their colourful imagery!

After this episode, the nawab was inclined to recite these few lines composed by himself in his own honour:

> Lagta nahin hai dil mera
> Is khooni jahaan main.
> Peeta hoon, peene do,
> Mujhe rakt e kafir ko.
> (I am not at peace
> In this murderous world.
> I drink, so let me drink,
> For, it is the infidel's blood I drink.)

*   *   *

Nawab Mian M. was up early the next morning and sent a flurry of messages to the snoring zamindar to wake up and join him for a pre-breakfast horse riding. Mian M. was an average rider but always sought to portray himself as a hussar of incredible horsemanship! To the nawab's dismay,

Zamindar Biltoo Khan preferred to ride women rather than horses and sent a message to this effect.

Nawab saheb would not relent so easily. Shiva and Rana had been saddled, and so would Zamindar Biltoo Khan be saddled with this morning run, come what may! Mian M. strode to the guest rooms and, shaking his friend by the shoulder, said, '*Ama, yaar*, Biltoo. Let us go for a short ride. It will give you a good appetite.'

Biltoo Khan, opening one eye, declared, 'Go away, Mian, I am enjoying the embrace of Mehrunnisa,' and started stroking his pillow.

'Mehrunnisa must be your churail. Now get up. I promise you an evening of good food and nautch by Tabassum Bai Naacheez from Barabanki.'

At the mention of Tabassum Bai Naacheez, Biltoo Khan woke up. After all, she was the most beautiful, voluptuous, and endearing *tawaif* in that side of the Gomti.

* * *

Shiva and Rana were both great horses in the stable of Mian M. Both were Marwari stallions in bay and chestnut colour respectively. Shiva was more spirited and was prone to showing off. At times, with the nawab on his back, he would just take off, leaping over stray dogs, chicken, and fowl, forcing the nawab to hold grimly on to the bridle and his saddle!

The nawab, therefore, preferred to ride on Rana, who was more docile and obedient. However, today, in deference to the zamindar's professed inexperience, Mian M. Ali was sitting upright on Shiva and was watching Biltoo Khan being pushed, pulled, and hefted on to the saddled Rana. Supported by syces on both sides, Biltoo Khan finally held the reins.

Having settled himself, Biltoo Khan, prone to theatrics, could not resist himself and stood up in the stirrups with a spine-chilling yell, 'Kreegaaah ayoooodeeee,' and the normally placid stallion just jumped in the air and, with a horrified neigh, shot off. It is said that dogs and horses are especially sensitive to the supernatural, and the ghoulish shriek of Zamindar Biltoo Khan, which had commenced in a baritone and ended in a falsetto, was indeed similar to the nocturnal crying of a depraved churail! Nawab saheb was also almost unseated as Shiva, spooked by the fiendish yell of zamindar saheb, had reared and was throwing his head around.

Biltoo Khan and Rana had cleared the compound in a whirl of dust and terrified yells. Mian M., fearing for the zamindar's limbs, gave chase on Shiva, roaring to his servants, 'Iska peechha kar.' Follow him.

The gaggle of munshis, syces, khidmatgaars, and jamadars assembled there joined the chase on foot, bicycles, and lung power. Very soon, an eagle circling above, drawn by the commotion, could see a white-clothed zamindar wrapped around the neck of his galloping chestnut, followed by a gesticulating nawab on his horse. And lagging behind but cycling furiously in the nawab's wake were the munshis and the khadims. The jamadars, still within the compound wall, seated comfortably on their haunches and smoking a bidi, were brandishing their brooms and roaring, 'Pakad le, pakad le, jaane na pai,' for the sake of pretence! Catch him, catch him, don't let him go.

The zenanas of the nawab's household, usually cloistered in their suites, were standing on their balconies and cheering the men on.

Rana, still not fully recovered from the fright of his rider's ghastly yell, was running hell for leather in a bid to get away from that thing. Unfortunately, that thing, the Zamindar Biltoo Khan, was hanging on to the mane of the stallion with both hands and was beseeching the horse to stop in Urdu, Farsi, Hindi, and English. His eyes, which were travelling vertically almost twelve inches on every stride of Rana, espied a huge lot of tree trunks stashed near the sugarcane field. And Rana seemed determined to hurdle over the logs!

Zamindar Biltoo Khan could no longer endure the rhythmic thumping of the saddle against his nether lands, and imagining the agony of a gargantuan thump against his testicles if Rana jumped, he sang 'Ammmiiiieeee' in the same primordial falsetto he had used before.

Rana could take no more. He just stopped. Nawab Mian M. Ali saw his friend Biltoo Khan being catapulted over the head of the stallion as free as a bird into the sugarcane field. Hurriedly jumping down from his horse, the nawab ran in the direction of the airborne zamindar.

Biltoo Khan had crash-landed on his belly, and the standing stalks of ripe sugarcane had not been kind to him. He was found lying on a bed of squashed sugarcane—some of which were indecently lodged in his groin, belly, and his armpit. Pitiful mewls were escaping from his lips.

The nawab, squatting by his friend's side, could not but remember a similar scene many years ago:

His grandfather, Nawab Mehboob Liyaqat Ali of Bilaul, was a hard-working nawab (for a change) and spent many hours in the agricultural fields, standing on the blade of the plough as the oxen pulled the plough across tracts under tillage. By standing on the blade, the nawab was able to get a deeper furrow, which translated in the seeds getting sown deeper into more fertile soil and, eventually, a better crop. Though the nawab was well off, he carried very little pretences of wealth. He had yet to buy a car. Even the tiny Ford Model T seemed expensive to him although nawabs of lesser means were charging around in Studebakers and Sunbeams. His preferred mode of transport was in palanquins.

On a warm summer day, he saw the village policeman perched on top of a thin contraption with two wheels travelling at a great speed. Hailing the policeman, Ranga Singh, he was told that the machine was called a cycle and could carry two people over large distances at a reasonable speed.

Nawab Mehboob L. Ali had to try that wonder machine! Havildar Ranga Singh explained to him, 'You just have to move your legs and steer by way of the handle.'

Supported by two farm hands, nawab saheb gathered his kurta pyjama together and slowly pedalled his way forward. Just ahead was a sharp slope which led to the lake. Nawab saheb, pumping his legs, steered this machine on to the muddy track where the cycle automatically started to gather speed and wobble around at a good clip. The nawab felt that he would be dislodged from his perch if he did not slow down. He called out to the cycle as he used to call out to his plough oxen, 'Eeyagh, eeyagh . . . Ruk, ruk.' Stop, stop.

No result.

'*Huzoor*, brake *lagaiye*, brake,' shouted Ranga Singh from afar. Sire, apply the brakes.

'Rukti kahe nahin hai, sasuri . . . Girayegi kya . . . Ruk, ruk.' Why don't you stop, devil? Will you make me fall? Stop, I say.

Still no result.

'Rukti hai ki kaan ke neeche do kantap jadoon? Naalayak, Naamakool . . . Ruk, saali, ruk . . . haiiyyaa.' Will you stop, or should I cuff you behind your ears? Useless, worthless heathen . . . stop!

And then he lamented as he went sailing headlong over the handlebars into a muddy ditch.

Nawab Mian M. closed his eyes and shuddered as he recollected his grandfather's ire. The enraged nawab had called for his shotgun, deaf to the pleas of Havildar Ranga Singh and had fired a number 12 cartridge at the mauled bicycle. One pea-size pellet had ricocheted from the bicycle rim and had found a home just below the nawab's left knee. The nawab howled, hobbled, and fell with the pellet precariously lodged in his calf.

The nawab muttered as he touched both his cheeks in penance, 'Lahoul vila kuvat.' By the might of Allah.

He dragged Zamindar Biltoo Khan from the sugar-coated embrace of the stalks. Zamindar Biltoo Khan was brought back to the nawab's haveli in a palanquin, face down. He had refused to be laid on his back as he could still feel the galloping thuds of Rana's saddle point on his butt! He was immediately ushered inside in a state of shock and was administered glasses of iced *khus ka sherbet* to reactivate his senses. Simultaneously, the khadims prepared an ointment made from lime, turmeric, and ginger and rubbed it on to the zamindar's aching backside and bruised ego!

Still in shock, Biltoo Khan decided to waive his breakfast. After a famously small lunch of nan, chicken *risaledar*, mutton stew, koftas, and pilaf, followed by delicious *zafrani kheer*, he retired for his afternoon siesta.

The evening saw Nawab Mian Muazzam Ali and Zamindar Biltoo Khan dressed in sparkling white kurtas, churidars, and golden nawabi *jooti*s (delicately crafted shoes in cloth and brocade). As Mian M. escorted the limping Biltoo Khan to the huge drawing room, their heady mix of colognes was enough to send the circling mosquitoes into a tizzy. Nawab saheb was resplendent, wearing a string of pearls with small rubies. The zamindar, not to be outdone, was weighed down with a heavy gold chain with many knots and twists.

The drawing room, or *jhumarkhana* (room of chandeliers) as it was locally known, was a huge rectangular hall almost forty feet long and twenty feet wide with six heavy doors and numerous small windows. All these doors and windows were wooden with small squares of coloured, multi-spectrum Belgian glass. There were huge cloth banners strung across the ceilings with long cords. It was the job of physically challenged villagers, unfit for any other labour, to tie one end of these cords to their fingers and pull the cloth banners—the native Indian fan at work!

Two sides of the room had cotton mattresses on the floor, covered in crisp white sheets, with rose petals strewn on them. Huge bolsters were strategically placed for the men to lean back on. Quite a few hookahs were placed at regular intervals, and a special intricately designed hookah made of pure silver with golden brocade wrapped on its pipe was kept in front of the mattress with red satin bolsters, where the nawab and his distinguished guest would be seated.

The nawab and the zamindar were preceded by Mehangoo, the valet who, suffused with the crackling 'sexcitement' of Tabassum Bai's imminent nautch and bursting with self-importance, was bowing low with salutations every few paces.

Zamindar saheb bravely limped along with quickened pace as they neared the jhumarkhana. They entered with a swish of curtains to a chorus of 'Salaam, huzoor' from the assembled guests as they rose in deference to the nawab.

The nawab, with a delicate wave of his hand, bade them to sit. He had eyes only for Tabassum Bai, who was bending low and, with bejewelled fingers, was touching her heart in salutation. The nawab acknowledged her salaams with a restrained smile and a slight inclination of his head.

Zamindar Biltoo Khan's eyes were at the furthest end of their sockets and were trying their best to get inside her cleavage! He was mesmerized by these two protuberances of Tabassum Bai. If these were the Himalayas, he would not mind climbing it! Tabassum, a veteran of numerous such bosom-stuck admirers, turned with an alluring smile towards him and gave a small delicate salaam. She was one of the finest dancers of classical Kathak, with a statuesque physique and very fair complexion.

Her large kohl-rimmed eyes were rumoured to mesmerize her lovers into total submission, and her delicate but well-fleshed limbs could send anyone into *jannat* (heaven)!

Biltoo Khan just managed to stop himself from fainting, and with a small hop, skip, and jump, he sat beside the nawab. The silver hookah was pulled closer—a sign for the festivities to begin.

Tabassum Bai of Barabanki gestured to her troupe of musicians, and they struck the first notes. Clad in a salmon-pink, gold, and sequin-embroidered lehnga (long skirt) with a bright-red satin coatee, she extended her right leg and marked time with her *ghungroo* (ankle bells). Slowly went the other leg, extended in a curl, thumping the floor in sweet cadence.

As the tempo increased, so did the intricate movements of Tabassum's legs. Nawab saheb forgot to pull on his hookah; Biltoo Khan Saheb had become immune to the pain in his body. The fifteen or so other gentlemen of dubious distinction were clearly myopic as they leaned forward to have a better glimpse of her rhythmic legs.

With every whirl, her skirt used to bellow and gather about her waist, and for a tiny second, her churidar-encased thighs would be visible to all present—and a wishful sigh would go up.

The nautch built up to a crescendo, and nawab saheb, in perfect sync with the twirling legs of Tabassum Bai, gave a mighty jerk of his head as the music peaked and stopped. Unfortunately, as he brought his hand and head down on the last beat, his dentures (made in England), which had been rattling inside his mouth, decided to fly loose and landed with a clack right at the painted toes of Tabassum Bai.

Zamindar Biltoo Khan, glancing at the puckered face of Nawab Mian M., let forth a huge guffaw, showering nawab saheb with little bits of betel nuts and freshly churned betel juice.

Nawab saheb, reduced to a toothless elf and embarrassed beyond sufferance, returned to the playing fields of Colvin Taluqdars' College. He turned to his right and threw himself on top of a startled Zamindar Biltoo Khan. His punches followed in quick succession on an already bruised Biltoo Khan. Lying underneath the bucking form of the nawab, Biltoo Khan raised his knee in self-defence.

As it always transpires, the rising knee, by some ancient ballistic trajectory calculations, consistently finds the scrotum!

Nawab saheb fell to the side, clutching his privates and spewing a steady stream of rustic abuses—some of them were traditional, but the majority were of new currency!

Zamindar Biltoo Khan, aware of the damage he had caused, quickly recovered and scrambled to his suite. Early next morning, as the muezzin called the faithful to prayers, Biltoo Khan, with a small bundle of essentials under his arm, slipped from the compound and melted into the early morning mist.

*   *   *

Nawab saheb recovered in a few days and sent for a new set of dentures. He shuddered every time he reflected on what could have been—from the nawab of Bilaul, he would have become the nawab without balls.

The Winding Road

Sheetal sat on a bench by the side of the road, her chin on her hands. She went there often, the Chapel Road, to enjoy the evening breeze in comparative solitude.

Nestled in the foothills of the Great Himalayas, cupping a lake in its palm, lay Nainital—hastily built and burgeoning yet on the tree-covered slopes of the Kumaon Hills. Pines and conifer trees were in autumn bloom again, and the snow-covered peaks of the Himalayas glistened further away on clear sunny days.

Sheetal let her thoughts wander to her happy home and family still residing in New Delhi. Oh, how she missed them—the familiar voice of her father, the sight of her mother with her knitting needles, her younger brother with his dangling white earphones and spiked hair. She smiled inwardly as the images clung to her with a vivid grip.

She was a frequent visitor to that part of Chapel Road, just off the main St Mary's College. The road was infrequently travelled after dusk. Sometimes she saw couples holding hands and walking by, lost in their own web of love;

maybe a lady with firewood on her head, hurrying home to light the kitchen fire; a cyclist at times, pedalling furiously home. The stretch of road was, at a bend, shielded from the glare of St Mary's College and St Joseph's Seminary, which lay a quarter mile in either direction from where she sat. The municipal street lamp had long ago lost its bulb to an angry wind and stood forlorn and desolate in its withered form.

She heard the crunch of footsteps on the dried leaves and twigs and pulled her shawl closer across her shoulders before looking around.

Yes, there he was again. Striding briskly towards her was the same man whom she had seen sitting on that same bench a few days ago. That day, she had hurried by, not wanting to stay there with a complete stranger on a barren stretch of road. The man had also not said anything, just watched her walk by with a sullen gaze. She had felt his cold stare on her back and again shuddered at the memory.

The steps slowed, and the man stopped for a brief second to look at her. With a heavy sigh, he chose a corner of the bench and sat down. Sheetal looked at him from the corner of her lowered eyes and quickly looked away. He was wearing the same clothes—the brown muffler, black sweater with white stripes on the arms, and green sneakers with dried mud on it. While she could not exactly put a finger on it, there was something about him which made her uneasy.

The man spoke, 'Hi, my name is Vishal. Have we met before?' The voice was ice-like in its coldness and seemed to come from far away.

'Sheetal. And I don't think we have met before,' she replied without much interest.

The man turned sideways to look at her, and she raised her eyes fearfully. A small frightened cry, like the yelp of a wounded animal, escaped her lips. The man's face was badly scarred with fresh wounds, and there was a deep hole in his forehead.

'I saw you passing by on Tuesday evening. I was sitting on this bench, and you just walked by. I saw you going past that bend.' He raised his arms and pointed in the distance. 'I thought of following you—I wish I had—then I would not have been shot dead on my way home. All for that lousy whore, Ginny!'

Paralysed with fear, Sheetal was almost in a faint. Another glance at his face, and she ran for her life. She cared not if her shawl caught in the brambles or if her denim shoes plucked as many thorns as they could. She just ran and ran.

She could hear his running footsteps getting closer and the laboured breathing through his bruised nose. She saw the small gate hanging ajar on its old pikes, and she just slammed through. Panting with exertion and relief, she sat against the wall and closed her eyes.

*　　*　　*

The man stood there, panting and heaving, with flecks of blood, spit, and foam, whistling through his broken teeth—he could not believe his eyes!

Draped across the tombstone in the evening light was the girl's pink shawl, partly concealing the inscription on the stone:

> Sheetal Gomes
> 14 March 1978 to 19 November 2004

'Well, well, fellow traveller,' chuckled the man as he turned into a bloody mist.

Exodus

Basement Parking
Ganga Deep Building
Juhu, Mumbai

The secretary of the Residents' Association brought the emergency meeting to order and tabled the first and only item on today's agenda.

'Mr President, senior members, and friends, we have convened here today to discuss a serious threat to our safety and health. I am sure you are aware of what we are referring to—the new occupant in flat no. 304.'

Having got everybody's attention, the secretary continued, 'The new occupant is a bachelor and works for an international airline.'

'Oh-ho, that explains his nocturnal activities,' said a wizened senior from flat no. 107. This senior had taken on the role of the building janitor and made it her business to keep an eye on the movements of all building residents.

'Yes, madam,' continued the secretary, 'the infernal noise coming from his flat is also an art that he has picked up from his many trips to Sweden, Bavaria, and Austria.'

'You call that godawful noise to be an art? Art, my foot. More like a humongous fart, if you ask me,' the resident editor of the monthly in-house magazine *Rattrap* spoke up. He presently resided in flat no. 302, directly opposite the erring resident.

'This humongous fart, as you have described it, is a much-revered form of singing in the Alpine regions. It is known as yodelling.' The Secretary looked around for appreciation. She had just gleaned the information while surfing the Net and was justifiably proud of her knowledge. Everyone in her class had always called her Rattoo for her ability to mug up answers.

The president, old and slightly deaf, looked up and, adjusting his glasses, said, 'We haven't got all day. Let us wrap up the business at hand.' He could not understand why the residents were making so much fuss over the new resident of flat no. 304!

'Old Mr Deaf cannot hear the hellish noise, hence he is not interested,' said a pretty young thin lady rat in a loud-enough voice for all the others to hear but to escape the audio parameters of the president.

There was a squeal of laughter, which quickly died as the president looked up and twitched his presidential whiskers in annoyance.

The secretary, adept at handling such diplomatic gaffes, quickly resumed, 'So, ladies and gentlemen, any comments on this issue?'

One hand came up. She had just given birth to twins and was even now trying to rock them to sleep. 'I say, this yodeller has to go. Although I stay two flights up, his constant wailing is too much for me to handle. Just as I put my twins to sleep, off comes his caterwauling through the walls. And damn, the twins are howling their heads off again!'

A fairly indignant resident of the eighth floor also spoke up, 'This man's singing, or wailing, is catastrophic for my family. All our stored cheese has mottled up. Must be the accursed sound waves of his yodelling.'

This was a serious environmental threat, and immediate action was required.

The president cleared his throat and said, 'Well, it is decided. We hereby pass a resolution condemning the sinful yodelling from occupant of flat no. 304 and agree to petition the society and the local MLA to rid us of this scourge. All in favour, raise your hands.'

The secretary counted and recorded. 'There are 117 members present—115 ayes, 2 abstentions. The motion is carried by majority.'

The president stood up and declared, 'We meet again after a week to review the progress. Stay calm, stay safe,' and with a slight bow, he walked out.

All the other rats too gathered their tails and marched off to their respective abodes.

* * *

The Same Evening
Flat No. 304
Ganga Deep Building

Jugal Kishore Khemraj was a tall strapping guy, fair in complexion, with a big mole just by his nose. He was fond of singing and cooking. Unfortunately, neither cooking nor singing was fond of him! To make matters worse, Jugal Kishore Khemraj, or JKK, considered himself to be a percussionist also of some repute and was inclined to reinforce his frequent bursts of singing with wanton clanging of kitchen utensils.

Lately, he had met a yodelling (*jodelling* in German) trio in a layover at Frankfurt and was instantly taken up by their yodelling skills. The yodellers had tried their best to explain the variations between the high head voice and the low chest voice but had given up after a few beers and annoyed customers at the roadside cafe where they were performing. That German, English, and Hindi were used in equal measure by the trainers and the trainee, had no effective effect on JKK. At the end of it all, he was convinced that the trick lay in bobbing his Adam's apple vertically, and that was what he subsequently concentrated on.

He spent the better part of a day hunting for *yodelling* DVDs and went back to Mumbai armed with his acoustic weaponry.

On a flight once, JKK was the galley purser and was tasked with announcing the flight safety regulations and drill. Every cabin crew on every airline knew that hardly 10 per cent of the passengers paid attention to the announcement being made. This flight was no exception, and JKK, viewing his somnolent audience, decided to bob his Adam's apple. The ensuing screech was such that it made the startled passengers reach for their oxygen masks.

Immediately after landing, JKK was surrounded by the airline security staff and marched off to the security centre. Upon pain of dismissal, JKK promised never to yodel in the skies again.

But today, he was back from a week-long itinerary of Mumbai–New York–Las Vegas–Honolulu–Frankfurt–Mumbai and was entitled to a four-day rest. He arched the hand towel over his head and, in his best Jimmy Rodger's twang, yodelled!

Two flights down under the stairwell, the resident cat gave premature birth to four kittens in sympathetic detonation to JKK's unnerving ululation!

* * *

Two Days Later
Common Hall
Ganga Deep Building

The Resident Welfare Association's meeting was in session, and Colonel (retired) Bahuguna was presiding.

'I am aware of the concerns raised by you and agree with all of it. However, there is something called the freedom of speech and expression guaranteed by our Constitution, and we cannot just lord it over some poor soul for trying to sing within the confines of his four walls. Each man's home is his castle!' finished Colonel Bahuguna in a grandiose manner.

'His four walls? The bloody duffer tried his stuff in the elevator one day, and short-circuited the electronic chip. The elevator got stuck on the second floor and would not budge. The doors also refused to open. We sent for the company service engineer, but our fellow, sick at being stuck inside for forty minutes, let out such a shriek of fear or annoyance that the doors opened with a rattle and this yodelling jerk toppled out. I refuse to get into an elevator if I see it hovering near the third floor,' panted Mr Vajpayee, a retired bureaucrat.

'Our maintenance charges will be hiked by the society if Mr Khemraj continues to practise his yodelling,' a retired school teacher added.

'I will sue Mr Khemraj, and I will sue the society if I am forced to live with this ghastly experience,' the building's resident lawyer, Mr Sohrab Gandhi, blustered.

'And sue him for what? For singing in his flat? For disturbing the peace? Mr Gandhi, your old Fiat makes more noise than ten yodellers combined' was the adversarial input from their own devil's advocate, Mr Pachauri. A semi-retired professor of sociology, he could be found most mornings loitering around the women's colleges of Mumbai. Good for his eyesight, he explained to anyone interested in his activities.

Mr Gandhi failed to rise to Mr Pachauri's bait. A snub was always better than a foolish argument!

Mrs Sharma of Kashi, Uttar Pradesh, was not to be ignored as she whined her grievance to the building residents, 'Ever since this new resident has come and has started making those ghoulish sounds, my children refuse to go to the park. They don't want to go to the grocery store in the basement also, afraid as they are of his singing.'

'Singing, my foot,' waded in the evergreen fighter Mr Vajpayee. 'More like an opera performance by a qualified jackass.'

Everybody sniggered at Mr Vajpayee's imagery.

Colonel Bahuguna looked at Mrs Nandoi with interest as she got up to speak. She was rumoured to be an air hostess with a famous airline and had just married a cardiac surgeon with whom she had become acquainted during a flight. She lived on the fifth floor and wore her sari many, many inches below her navel. Looking at her awesome navel, Colonel Bahuguna slowly understood the attraction powers of the sun's black hole!

Mrs Nandoi glanced coyly at Colonel Bahuguna and opined, 'See, his singing is a nuisance, I agree. In fact, at times, my crockery falls off the shelves when Mr Khemraj throws his voice out of the windows. But other than his yodelling, I see no reason to stack up against him.'

Mr Debara, a Parsi car showroom owner, well into his seventies, listened attentively to the exchanges. He plainly loved Mr Khemraj as, ever since his moving in, Mr Debara had experienced an absolute improvement in his constipation. Now, every morning, he tried to synchronise his bowel eviction with the bathroom rites of JKK, when he was at his best with his yodelling practice. This phenomenon must have a scientific reason—probably the yodelling notes, especially in the triad, tickled a funny nerve in the intestine, which in turn increased peristalsis, and lo, quick eviction! This free yodelling laxative was worth keeping, surmised Mr Debara.

'I agree with Mrs Nandoi. There is no reason to bring in the heavy artillery against Mr Khemraj. Mrs Nandoi, will you please help me in drafting a "soft" letter to Mr Khemraj? We can do it tomorrow afternoon, hmm?' Colonel Bahuguna with his presidential address brought the lid down finally on the kettle.

*   *   *

Open Car Parking
11 p.m.
Ganga Deep

The three *bhoot*s (male ghosts) and one *churail* (female ghost) sitting on the roofs and bonnets of the parked cars had covered their ears and closed their eyes as JKK pranced past them, singing an improbable Franzl Lang number. Franzl Lang was the undisputed king of yodelling, and JKK was a sorry entertainer. The Bavarian yodel that JKK was trying to replicate was mostly coming across as the post-orgasmic bleat of a she goat.

The assembled ghosts followed the exit course of JKK through half-closed eyes peering from behind split fingers. They removed their fingers from their eyes only when they saw him enter the elevator.

This place was becoming too dangerous for them. Their cemetery and burning ghats were much safer!

They glanced at one another and then shot off to sit on the electric poles outside the compound wall.

*   *   *

Two Days Later
Basement Parking
Ganga Deep Building

'This emergency meeting is called to order. Madam Secretary, please read for the records.' The president was all business today.

The secretary stood up and announced, 'This emergency meeting has been called to decide the plan of action required to combat the continuous audio assault on us over the last two days. We have several complaints from our members. Please come forward with your comments.'

A fat rat residing in flat no. 202 with a medical physician and his wife got up, and after adjusting his glasses, he began, 'Mr President and dear friends, it pains me to present our series of complaints against the serial offender residing in 304.' He put his left hand inside his trouser pocket and scratched discreetly.

'This fiend in a human's body is not of this planet, of that I am sure. I have seen many patients in my lifetime, both here and on my occasional trips to the hospital with the good doctor, but never have I come across anything as vile as this.' Scratch, scratch.

A lady rat mother of a young rat cut in, 'This yodeller is barbaric. He is destroying our language and our culture. Now my son is so influenced by the idiot's seismic churning of sounds that he is forgetting our national traditional language of Ratspeak.' And so saying, she cuffed her son behind his ears.

The medical rat took stage again. 'This man, this devil with the banshee wail has absolutely no consideration for others. He starts bawling at the drop of a hat and does not follow the acoustic startle protocol (ASP), which is so necessary for the good health and longevity of rats. The other day, I was dozing atop the curtain rod when this damned yodeller just let forth. I was so startled that I almost fell into an open vessel of boiling milk.'

'Ooohhh.' The rats shuddered collectively.

'Therefore, as an advanced medical practitioner, it is my professional opinion that, in the interests of our good health, longevity, and our future generations, we must find a safer habitat. We must move!' The medical rat sat down to a sustained round of applause.

The president stood up and, leaning on the upturned soap box, said, 'In the interests of our rat race, we must move. And move soon! As this is a historic decision, please raise your tails and be counted. Let not the future generations of rats say that we dithered while our cheese mottled! Secretary.'

The secretary looked at the sea of quivering tails and gladly announced, 'All present voting for the motion.'

The president puffed up his chest and almost fell off the soap box as he said, 'We march tonight!'

*   *   *

That Same Night

The bhoots and the churail sitting on the electricity poles outside the compound saw the departing contingent of rats and chortled. 'Sensible buggers!'

Travesty of Justice

February 2009
Fatehpur Central Jail

The deputy jailer looked outside into the jail courtyard from his first-floor office window. The same routine—at 4 p.m. sharp, the convicts would slowly trickle into the courtyard for their evening exercise regimen. This was part of the jail protocol, and no one was exempt.

The convicts would fall in their respective block formations A, B, C, D, E . . . and wait for their evening attendance. Jails were full of attendance schedules, much like schools—early morning attendance, breakfast attendance, work detail attendance, lunch attendance, tea attendance, evening attendance, dinner attendance, and finally, barrack night attendance!

The deputy jailer glanced at me and asked, 'Tell me, Vivek, Janardhan Singh is quite a loner, isn't he? I never see him mixing readily with anyone, and that is pretty strange, considering he has been here for, what, close to twelve years now?'

I walked over and stood next to the deputy jailer. Most of the convicts were walking around the perimeter of the courtyard while a few were doing freehand exercises. The younger ones were playing basketball on the court made towards the dining hall block. The volleyball nets had been removed, for more often than not, it ended up with the two teams having a go at each other.

I was the medical officer at the jail. Convict no. 142445, Janardhan Singh, had at times of staff crunch helped me out in the jail dispensary as he was educated and seemed soft spoken in this crowd of thugs, murderers, and criminals of every shape and size. As he spent hours poring over my hastily scribbled prescriptions and measuring out tablets, syrups, and capsules from the mini pharmacy unit that we had within the jail premises, most of the medical staff at the dispensary liked him. We always made sure that our 11 a.m. as well as the 3.30 p.m. tea and refreshments were made available to him.

Today, I saw him again sitting on his favourite stone step, resting his head on his bent arm and gazing vacuously into the red brick wall. A few walkers stopped and murmured greetings to him as he sat, and he acknowledged them with a shy smile.

'Yes, he is a loner, all right. Doesn't mix much with the other chaps, but stays clear of trouble. Or maybe trouble stays clear of him!' I smiled at my own witticism. The deputy jailer smiled too and sat down.

'If the story about him is true, then even Lakhan Singh will not get too close to him. It is said that he had chopped the body into several miniscule parts before throwing it into the river. And the eye witness had said that he was doing it with absolute equanimity!' observed the jailer.

Lakhan Singh was our most famous inmate—a dacoit with an armed gang of twenty-five to thirty dreaded criminals. He was the scourge of the Chambal and carried a bounty of one lakh of rupees on his head. His infatuation with a shop owner's daughter and recurrent visits to her house in Banda in disguise had proved to be his Waterloo. A police informant who owed money to the shop owner— or Lala as he was referred to in the village—had secretly informed the local police.

Such was Lakhan Singh's notoriety and pervasive fear that the local thana had sat over this information for several weeks before seeking assistance from the neighbouring district forces. Once assured of heavy police bundobust, the local thana laid a trap during a local festival and arrested Lakhan Singh as he went disguised as a bangle seller!

I squinted against the setting sun and watched Janardhan doze off. No one interacting with him could ever believe that this was a man charged and convicted of first-degree murder—and that too with an axe!

***

A Few Years Ago
Medical Dispensary
Fatehpur Central Jail

We were relaxing with our mid-morning chai and samosas when my eyes fell on Janardhan Singh sitting quietly in a corner with his glass of tea and piping hot samosas on a torn-off sheet of old newspaper. Something within told me that there was more to Janardhan's story than plain, wilful murder.

I could not resist and blurted out, 'Janardhan!' Maybe my tone was sharper than I had intended.

'Yes, sir' came the frightened response as he got up immediately, putting his tea and samosas on the ground and wiping his hands on the seams of his cream-coloured pyjamas.

'No, no, relax! May I ask you something?'

'Of course, Doctor Sahib,' he said with a resigned air.

'Listen, you don't have to tell me if you don't want to, but I would like to know the true story.' I was leaning forward in my chair.

'The true story?' Janardhan looked at me with pained eyes, and then a disdainful smile spread on his face. 'You must believe in what my file says and what the hon'ble court declared.'

Hon'ble court? I thought. This was the first time I had ever heard a convict refer to the court as hon'ble, and especially after being awarded the death penalty.

The prisoners had a vast vocabulary of vituperative words in several languages and dialects, but never *hon'ble*!

I looked more closely at Janardhan Singh.

Five feet ten inches or so, with a fair complexion and silver-grey hair, he had a sturdy build which even the last twelve or thirteen years in prison had not managed to quell. His eyes earlier were clear and bright, but now they were dulled with pain and resignation. Crow's feet had formed around his eyes, but his gentle demeanour had still not been compromised by the criminalized environment of the jail precincts. Smiles were few and far between.

Janardhan looked up again and smiled at my inquisitiveness. 'It is a long story, sahib! Maybe some other day?'

'We have all the time in the world, Janardhan! The OPD is weak today, thank God.'

'Yes, sir, because today is Sunday. Tomorrow will be full of stomach- and headaches.' It was a fact. Mondays had the highest turnout of patients as they wanted to extend their weekend by one more day.

Janardhan looked at me quizzically, and I nodded with a smile.

He sighed and, turning his head towards the green curtained window, said, 'From where should I begin, Doctor Sahib?'

'Right from the very beginning, Janardhan.'

*　*　*

'It was the summer of 1994, and I was posted as a junior engineer in the Irrigation Department at Gonda as a section in charge of the Ghaghra Elevated Canal Project funded by the World Bank. I was temporarily based at Mewati, a small village about forty-two kilometres west of Gonda, while my wife, Rupa, and my two daughters, aged seven and nine, were staying in the Hydel Colony at Gonda district headquarters.

'I had a staff of about a hundred and fifty–odd people, including labourers from Bilaspur, technical staff, maintenance crew, and drivers of all kinds of vehicles. We had erected temporary structures for accommodation as well as mess canteens for the accumulated workers. We were all within a compound made of barbed wire and tin sheets stretched around the undulating scrubland. There were numerous reports of hyenas and wolves sulking around our campsite. The labourers were afraid that the hyenas and the wolves would harm their children.

'We doubled the security around the camp and encouraged the casual labour to move in groups after sunset. The work progressed at a good pace and well within our time schedule. This was a prestigious project worth over 4,200 crores, of which approximately 1,400 crores were meant for our divisional office and its related work.

'Our division was looked after by a superintending engineer, Mr B. N. Srivastava, who was a frequent visitor to our site for inspections as well as with big and small politicians. This was a flagship project of the Uttar Pradesh government, and it was believed that its successful completion would give the UP government more leverage in future funding from the IMF and the World Bank!

'All was going well until one day when we heard rumours about a big embezzlement being detected in our division.'

'Big? How big, Janardhan?' I interjected.

'The figures being thrown around were of Rs.250 crores, but no one knew for sure. All that we knew were hearsay and rumours. Work progressed, but to tell you frankly, our rhythm had been disturbed.

'Then one day came rumours that the funds fraud was detected in our section of the canal project. We were flummoxed, for although there had been some instances of pilfering of iron rods and cement bags, nothing alarming had occurred. And such instances of pilferages were common to all sites. In fact, in desolate sites, even jeeps and heavy equipment went missing.'

Janardhan stopped and looked at me—he was probably trying to search for some form of understanding or empathy in my eyes. I looked calmly back at him and said, 'And then what happened, Janardhan?'

'As I was saying, stealing was common. In fact, the superintending engineer of Mirzapur was once kidnapped by the Naxalites and was released only after fifteen days of captivity. The police were helpless, and it was only with the intervention of some politicians from Jharkhand that the Naxals consented to release the superintending engineer. The SE opted for VRS immediately after this, but that was understandable.'

He stopped again and then, with a sigh, continued, 'Early one morning, there was a rush of senior departmental officers with a posse of policemen in tow. They cordoned off the administrative and account sections and, within two hours, were gone with all the files—accounting and procurement vouchers, labour pay sheets . . . everything. We were just mute spectators to the whole drama.

'Needless to say, work came to a standstill at the site from that day onwards as all activities were put on hold, pending investigations. The casual labourers engaged on daily wage basis were the first to go. They had to find work every day to survive. Then the contractors with the heavy equipment left. They had to pay the monthly instalments on these machines and could not spend weeks or months idling by.'

'What happened to you all?' I enquired.

'Well, we had still not been transferred, so we continued to stay at the site. But our visits to Lucknow head office increased. In a few days, I felt a palpable change in the attitude of my colleagues. They started avoiding me and would glance away if I looked towards them. They would deliberately turn their backs on me if they saw me coming their way.

'I could handle it no longer and one day accosted Shyam Babu, a sectional clerk, in the paan shop outside. We had both joined the Irrigation Department around the same time, and our first posting was at Lalitpur, near Jhansi, on the Sharda Sahayak canal project. "Shyamji, what is going on here?" Shyamji made as if to move away, but I caught him by his arms. "You have to tell me, or I will go mad with anxiety. Please, Shyam babu,"' I had pleaded.

'Shyam babu just looked at me and, with a shake of his head, moved away. From his murmured answer, I could just make out that I was also under suspicion for embezzlement. Like a man possessed, I visited every senior officer and sat with every section head to glean some more information but to no avail. It was difficult for me to accept the fact that I could ever be accused of financial impropriety. Those who knew me in the department were equally convinced of my innocence, although a few troubled souls had also remarked that I was intelligent enough to make a huge financial killing.'

Looking down at the glass of tea cupped in his hands, he continued, 'I applied for medical leave and went back to Gonda to be with my wife, Rupa, and with my daughters. I had no wish to burden Rupa with my impending troubles and, hence, tried to maintain as normal a demeanour as I could under the circumstances. But you just cannot deceive your wife. Rupa saw through my act and kept asking me the cause of my worries.' Having said this, Janardhan looked up briefly at me, and I could see his eyes clouded with unshed tears.

'Look, Janardhan, you don't have to continue if you don't want to. I know you are innocent.' My heart went out to this fellow human being separated from his wife and daughters for a crime which he may *not* have committed.

'No, Doctor Sahib, somebody has to know. So anyway, one day I received a message to meet the superintending engineer, Mr Srivastava, at the Mewati project site and resume duties. Relieved, I immediately left for the project site by an official jeep of the Irrigation Department. Srivastava Saheb was already there, waiting for me. After welcoming me back, he asked to be shown around the site. I enquired if my immediate superior, Mr Sharma, the executive engineer, would be joining us, but the superintending engineer said that Mr Sharma would be joining over the next few days.

'I took him around the now-desolate site and showed him the stores of cement bags, sand, and steel which we still retained. The cement had mostly set, but the sand and steel were in good condition. We walked towards the elevated area where the canal dykes had been dug and cemented. As we reached near the slippery, rocky bank of the Ghaghra, Mr Srivastava stunned me by quietly telling me that I was implicated in a financial fraud amounting to almost 147 crores and that a departmental enquiry would be set up next Monday. I was rendered speechless for a moment, and then I protested vehemently.'

With downcast eyes, Janardhan continued, 'By now, my mental equilibrium had collapsed, and catching the superintending engineer by the collar, I spun him around and threw him on to the rocks. He lay there, looking at me with fearful eyes, and I resisted the urge to pick up a boulder and smash his head in. Confused, miserable, and scared, I just ran. I do not remember how I reached the main road, but I remember flagging down a Bolero and squeezing in with the other passengers.'

I was riveted to his narrative and ignored the clock striking twelve.

'That night, around midnight, the police arrived.' Janardhan looked at me with anguished eyes. 'I was pulled out of my house and thrown into the police jeep. I kept asking for the charges against me. "You will know at the police station" was all they said. My wife was roughly pushed away, and I just saw them standing near the steps, crying and clinging on to one another.' His voice was a whisper now.

'That night, I was interrogated for almost seven hours for the murder of Mr B. N. Srivastava, superintending engineer. I was arraigned the same night, and produced before the sessions magistrate the next day. I was remanded to fifteen days of police custody and then put on trial.

'The subsequent days of trial and prison were just a blur for me. The police had built up a case of murder against me based on my last interaction with the SE. An old farmer tending his sheep along the far bank had seen two men scuffling and then one being thrown to the ground on the rocks. I know that part is true. But then came the embellishments—the farmer lied that he had seen one person wielding a huge knife, like a *chapar* [chopper], and repeatedly hacking at the person lying defenceless on the rocks! SE sahib's driver and a few other workers also corroborated the story that I had taken the SE towards the riverbank and had not returned. In fact, both of us had not returned. The forensics unit of the police nailed the final nail in my coffin when they provided evidence that the copious amount of blood present on the rocks were indeed of the SE as it matched the B negative profile of the slain SE.' Janardhan was slumping against the wall now, his back arched.

'My wife fought tooth and nail to prove my innocence. She sold off most of her jewellery to pay the lawyers. We had bought a small plot on Faizabad road to build our own house, but it was sold to raise the money for bribing the sessions judge to grant me relief and procure bail. Nothing happened. I was given a death sentence by the sessions court on account of committing a first-degree murder in an inhuman, heinous manner. The high court, in appeal, commuted the sentence to life imprisonment. So here I am.' A resigned shrug, and then Janardhan was silent.

'But what was the motive? An overpowering motive is required to frame murder charges.' My professional instincts were taking over.

'SE Sahib was the main accused in the financial scam. And I supposedly was his point man in the project here, siphoning off the funds through fake procurement and payment vouchers.'

'Then you must have been convicted on two counts— firstly, for the murder of Srivastava, and secondly, for embezzlement,' I queried.

'No, Doctor Sahib, the department could not prove my involvement in the fraud as none of the suspect vouchers or procurement orders carried my original signatures. They were initialled in my name but were clearly different. Also, on some of the voucher dates, I was on leave! The high court took a lenient view and absolved me from all counts of larceny. It also mitigated the murder charges from first degree to third degree, committed under circumstances leading to severe mental distress, and reduced my sentence to life imprisonment.'

'Wow, what a journey, Janardhanji.' There was a sudden respect in my eyes for this fellow of fortitude.

'Yes, but I have lost my wife, my daughters, my happiness, my faith in God. I abhor the name of justice and good deeds. I hate life.'

'Where are your wife and children? I have not seen them coming here.'

'I told my wife not to bring our children here. They were nine and seven when I was arrested. They would be almost twenty-one and nineteen today. I would rather they carry memories of our happy times together.' Janardhan's eyes were swimming in tears, and voice choked.

My own eyes were stinging with tears, and a lump had grown in my throat. I slowly got up and, patting Janardhan on his shoulder, went into the adjacent room to check the surgical supplies.

*   *   *

February 2009
Deputy Jailer's Office
Fatehpur Central Jail

'This, sir, is the complete story of Janardhan Singh,' I finally closed my narrative of the last half an hour.

'Remarkable,' intoned the jailer as he revolved a pencil between his fingers.

*   *   *

12 November 2012
Front Page, *Indian Post*
New Delhi Edition

The right-hand side column on the front page declared a headline in size 24 font.

Dead Man Commits Suicide!
By Special Correspondent

Late last night, a body was discovered in room no. 136 of Hotel Ragini at Kota, Rajasthan, by the room service boy who had gone to enquire for dinner. This guest had been staying in this hotel alone for the last two months.

A suicide note was found by the body, which identified the deceased as one Mr

B. P. Srivastava, former superintending engineer of the UP Irrigation Department. Interestingly, the deceased had been assumed murdered, although his body was never found, and as per police records, a subordinate officer, Janardhan Singh, was found guilty of third-degree murder and sentenced to life imprisonment. He is currently languishing in the Fatehpur Central Jail.

The suicide note also acknowledges the full complicity of the deceased in the infamous Rs.147 crores scam of the UP Irrigation Department in the early nineties. In his suicide note, the deceased has asserted that he was hand in gloves with some very powerful politicians and had managed to funnel out almost 150 crores over a period of thirty months from the departmental funds.

The deceased has declared that he has lost his will to live, having lost his wife and only son in September this year. The suicide note also describes in detail the peregrinations of the deceased over the last twenty years since his feigned death.

Possibly, in an act of repentance, the deceased has informed the various account numbers of several banks in which a large part of the booty is stashed.

Now, this brings us to the question of who will reimburse Janardhan Singh for the almost fifteen years spent in jail for a crime he did not commit.

*   *   *

13 November 2012
5.20 a.m.
Fatehpur Central Jail

With my hands covered in blood, I went running from barrack A to the jailer's office. There was a crowd of convicts standing outside, but they silently made way for me as I went rushing towards the administrative block.

The deputy jailer was standing by his desk and reading an official-looking paper. Two lawyers accompanied by a sub-inspector were also in the room.

'Sir,' I exclaimed with anguish, 'Janardhan Singh has cut his wrists. He is dead.'

The deputy jailer looked at me with stricken eyes and slumped on his chair, for lying on his desk were the release orders for convict no. 142445, Janardhan Singh, son of Ram Gopal Singh of Soraon, District Allahabad.

*   *   *

The Supreme Court
Foyer
9 a.m.

An early judge, walking briskly down the main foyer of the supreme court, glanced at the Lady Justice perched atop a decorative pedestal. Something was amiss—yes, the scales were tilted to one side!

Motioning to his personal secretary, he gestured towards the lopsided scales. The secretary, with early morning alacrity, spoke to a uniformed policeman on the way.

Within five minutes, a maintenance crew was cleaning the debris of bird poop from the tilted scales of justice.

The Hermit

December 1890
Sher Ghati, near Sasaram, Bihar

I must rest my tired limbs now. For over 140 years, I have seen the pillage of my country, the merciless killing of our brethren, and the endless guile of the *firangis*, their assertion over most of central, north, and east India after the Battle of Plassey, the death of 10,000 British soldiers and almost a lakh of my countrymen in the cholera pandemic, the demise of East India Company in the hands of the British Crown, the wigged Warren Hastings as the first governor general, the treachery of our native brothers in joining the British Imperial Army for a few annas and rupiah, their strutting around in the scarlet, white, and gold of the *firangi sipahi*.

But most of all, I remember the carnage and misery following the Sepoy Mutiny. As I sat under the peepul tree, oh, what courage and grief I saw! Remembering those few months of unbridled terror through my own eyes, I often cursed myself and my sadhana (spiritual practice) for this accursed gift of envisioning from afar all that I set my mind to.

Now in my 140th year, I still cannot close my eyes, for the images, like distant relatives, keep visiting with no respite. I carry a heavy cross and a matter which I can never reveal! If ever the fact is disclosed, Hindustan will never be the same again!

I want no silver plaques or gold mohurs or for people to fall at my feet. I want no revenge, no more bloodshed, no patriotic chants or battle flags unfurled. I just want to close my eyes and smoothly cross the Great Divide.

June 1858
Small Hillock, near Gwalior

I have been sitting here and watching through my accursed eyes the fate of Jhansi and its pitiful existence. Not that I wish to, but I cannot ignore what envelops the mind and creeps into your body through every single pore and breath.

My eyes remain fixed, but my mind takes me back five years in time—to when a jubilant Raja Gangadhar Rao of Jhansi and his beautiful queen, Laxmi Bai, were expecting their first child. For a few months, even the ever-ailing raja had shown signs of improving health and was again taking interest in matters of state.

Jhansi Ka Kila, 1853

Raja Gangadhar Rao is bedridden with fever and bouts of melancholia, for he cannot reconcile himself to the death of his four-month-old son, who was christened Damodar Rao. The rani also is consumed with grief, and no amount of ministrations by Moti Bai or Sunder–Munder can get her out of her rings of wretchedness.

Fearing that Jhansi may slip out of the ruling dynasty in case Raja Gangadhar Rao succumbs to his illness and the British Crown enforces the Doctrine of Lapse, the royal couple, still in throes of misery, adopts the son of a distant relative from the same Newelkar clan as the current raja of Jhansi. The adoption was done as per Hindu rites in the presence of the royal court as well as the British political agent and the British garrison commander.

Raja Gangadhar Rao passed away soon thereafter in November 1853 under the illusion that the queen empress would honour the fidelity of the royal court of Jhansi to the Crown and would be fair to the widowed queen and their adopted son.

Nothing could have been further from the truth. The rani has been forced to vacate the fort and confine herself to the rani mahal. Her rightful claims to the Crown, titles, and treasure of Jhansi have also been snatched by the British, and she is now given an annual purse of Rs.60,000 for her maintenance. No amount of representation from the rani to the Queen Empress Victoria or her representatives has brought any relief.

During this period, the Queen Empress Victoria is productively engaged in producing nine children with her consort, Prince Albert, though she always professes a deep dislike for pregnancy and childbirth.

The local populace of Jhansi are enraged at the injustice meted out to their beloved rani, and their resentment results in several small uprisings against the British garrison at Jhansi.

The personal intervention of Rani Laxmi Bai, who is still hopeful of a peaceful transfer of her rights and titles, saves the British forces and their families on more than one occasion.

However, this mosaic of administrative treachery, British greed and insensitivity, reluctance of a young widowed queen to take up arms, and a limited treasury is soon to be shattered.

Jhansi simmers.

May 1857
Small Hillock, near Gwalior

Sitting in front of my hermit's cottage on a small hillock strewn with shisham trees and boulders, I see the Indian sepoys of the British Indian Army resisting the British imposition of new cartridges greased with cow and pig fat. The first shots fired on the Meerut cantonment parade ground ring the death knell of the end of British rule in India ninety years from now.

But who will believe me today if I foretell the future?

November 1857 to 15 June 1858
Jhansi Ka Kila, Jhansi

Rani Laxmi Bai has been busy assembling a small army of loyal subjects, including women, to take on the might of the British Army marching towards Jhansi after curbing the rebellion at Allahabad and Cawnpore. Many of the Indian regiments, including the famed Bengal native infantry, have been disbanded, and its Indian sepoys discharged in disgrace. The small neighbouring kingdoms of Orchha and Datia are instigating the British through secret missives and personal representation regarding the massacre of the British officers and their families, numbering thirty-two, on the pretext of safe passage granted by the rani of Jhansi. The British government at Calcutta, smarting under the casualties and atrocities committed on the British, is only too willing to believe and act upon the canards.

Of the ten gates in Jhansi Fort, four have been permanently bricked to neutralize the chances of breach. Only six are used—Khanderao Dwar, Datia Darwaza, Jharna Dwar, Orchha Gate, Laxmi Dwar, and Chand Dwar. The main commanders of the rani's army—Basharat Ali, Dost Khan, Diwan Raghunath Singh, and Diwan Jawahar Singh—have been augmenting the defences and ammunition. Training is being imparted to the musketeers and sowars (mounted troops) in preparation of the impending war.

The twenty-two ladies in waiting to the rani, led by the inseparable Sunder–Munder, Kashi Bai, Moti Bai, and Jhalkari Bai are training other 700 women recruits in the use of swords, spears, and small musketry. Another group of almost 1,100 middle-aged women are engaged in the supply and storage of arms and ammunition at strategic points. They are also charged with the task of replenishing ammo and victuals in battle situations.

The fort's main cannons, numbering about thirty-two, are strategically placed on ramparts towards Orchha and Banda, from where the attack is anticipated. Cannoneers have also pulled out the smaller batteries of cannons and spread them along the minor ramparts and turrets to continue the fusillade when the bigger cannons are being reloaded and rearmed.

The two main cannons of Jhansi Fort, Kadak Bijlee and Bhawani Shanker, under cannoneer commanders Ghulam Ghaus Khan and Lala Bhau Bakshi, have been propitiated with offerings of marigold flowers, honey, and incense sticks.

The regular army of about 1,000 men has been augmented by rebel sepoys and mutineers, dacoits of Bundelkhand, Rajputs, Mussalmans, and every disgruntled native drawn to the rani's saffron flag of Jhansi and liberation. The army now stands at 7,000 soldiers and 1,200 sowars.

Rani Laxmi Bai of Jhansi cuts a resolute figure in her sowar's armour as she rides the fort's parapet on her beloved horse, Badal.

March 1858 to 18 June 1858
Small Hillock, Kotah-ki-Serai, near Gwalior

Divinity has not been kind to me in rewarding me with these bedevilled eyes. Why can I not see what normal humans see? Why must I be forced to see what my mind seeks? I have absolutely no interest or concern in the British besiegement of Jhansi Ka Kila. But at times, I do think of the young rani, widowed at such an early age and vulnerable to all the slights and adversity of time. And then my eyes, trapped in their own ruination, take me there to be like a fly on the wall to observe, store, and chronicle for the generations to come who shall remain oblivious to my plight.

Let this be a warning to all mendicants: be careful what you wish for! My heart bleeds for the rani as I watch the

British forces under Major General Hugh Rose besiege the Jhansi Fort in early March. The calls to surrender from the British evoke a taut and acerbic reply from the young rani: 'Main apni Jhansi nahin doongi!' I shall not surrender my Jhansi!

The first shots are fired on 24 March 1858, and Jhansi answers with a resounding fusillade of cannons into the gathered British forces. The general disperses his troops on both flanks and moves his cannons towards Orchha Dwar and Laxmi Dwar.

Both sides trade cannonballs. The Jhansi cannons are capable of handling cannonballs weighing from five seers to sixty-five seers as they are placed in situ. The British forces are carrying lighter artillery, but their sustained fire on particular dwars and sections of the wall is taking their toll. The fort walls come close to being breached, but the ready crowd of Jhansi citizens, briefed in advance, rush with their rocks, boulders, lime, and burnt hessian rope to cement the walls.

On 31 March, fearing a collapse of the weakened Orchha Dwar, it is decided that the rani, with a small force, shall try to escape.

As darkness descends, two women in armour embrace. Jhalkari Bai, a close confidante of the rani, is wearing the rani's armour and her signature white pagri under her helmet. She has tied a bundle on her back, resembling a child in harness.

With an escort of about 120 sowars, she races out of the crumbling Orchha Dwar with the saffron flag of Jhansi fluttering in the hands of the adjacent sowar, crosses the moat, and then immediately wheels left. A small squadron of British cavalry, entrusted to deal with exactly this eventuality, gives chase.

Cries of 'Pakdo, pakdo, Rani bhaag rahi hai' ('Catch them, the rani is escaping') galvanizes the Crown troops into action. More riders join the chase and race away into the undulating plains towards Lalitpur. After a short battle, Jhalkari Bai, deliberately distancing herself from her sowars, wheels around for a last stand. With her face covered with a part of her pagri, she wields the swords with both hands. The fight is fierce and uneven and quickly ends when five cavalry troops, led by Captain Page, plunge their sabres into her. Captain Page also fires his pistol at her head from point-blank range. She falls and is immediately surrounded by the rejoicing troops.

They put her inert body on her horse and, with a British soldier holding the reins, race back to their camp, whooping with joy. The remnants of her escort break away from the engagement and ride back towards the fort.

No one chases them as the rani has been killed. Rani Laxmi Bai, with tears streaming down her oval face, and Damodar, clinging to her back, rode out silently from the Khanderao Dwar. Before leaving, she pays obeisance at the small shrine of Shree Batuk Bhairav near the royal tank, where she bathes every day. Her retinue was small, just a few trusted commanders, including Diwan Raghunath Singh, Diwan Jawahar Singh, Ghulam Ghaus Khan, Basharat Ali, Dost Khan, Khuda Baksh, Lala Bhau Bakshi, Ganpat Rao, and a few others. Her female attendants and compatriots were Moti Bai, Sunder–Munder, Kashi Bai, and four others.

I see her stop a *kos* (two miles) from the fort and gaze with wistful eyes at the now silent fort standing majestically atop the Bangira hill.

She throws a look of repulsive contempt at the British camp celebrating her death and urges her horse, Badal, into a canter. She goes faster after clearing another kos to hide the dust and clatter of her retinue.

I can see her now reaching Kalpi, a ride of ninety-three miles in twenty-four hours! Her trusted horse, Badal, unable to go further, has been changed for a new horse, Pari, at the village of Akori, about twenty miles and four hours back. Her other followers have also changed their horses for fresh ones.

She meets up with Tatya Tope at Kalpi and is astonished to see him leading 20,000 armed troops. They have laid siege to Kalpi but not for long. Soon enough, the British attack in force, and the rani is made to flee to Gwalior, along with Tatya Tope and a major portion of his troops.

Jayajirao Scindia, the ruler of Gwalior, resists the entry of the rebels, but I can see his troops deserting him and joining the rebels. Cries of 'Har Har Mahadev' and 'Rani Laxmi Bai ki Jai' rent the air as saffron and mustard-yellow pennants sway in the air. Scindia flees to Agra.

It is dusk, and I can see her entrusting little Damodar Rao into the hands of Kashi Bai and Ganpat Rao. 'Take care of him, for he is the future of Jhansi. You swear upon your rani to protect him with your lives and reach him safely to the court of the Peshwa at Bithoor. Now, go!'

With a soft kiss on the forehead of the sleeping Damodar, she sends them away, trailed by a dozen attendants.

18 June 1858
Kotah-ki-Serai, near Phool Bagh, Gwalior

From my vantage point, I see the rani clad in a sowar's armour, leading her small detachment of about 110 sowars from the fort's main gate. She wheels left towards the British cavalry troops of the Eighth King's Royal Irish Hussars. Her trusted lieutenants and bodyguards close in around her as she races flat out at the enemy. The hussars, charging in close formation, are scattered at the ferocity of the rani's charge. The rebels cut deep into the hussar ranks, but then at a shouted order from their troop leader, Captain Heneage, they close ranks and are able to cut off the forward ranks of the Indian horsemen from their main body.

The rani, leading the charge, is deep into the hussar ranks and is shielded on the flanks by Dost Khan and Basharat Ali. She is holding the reins between her teeth and wielding swords in both hands. Pari, not used to battle, is skittish and prancing around wildly.

Pari neighs and rears back, almost throwing the rani to the ground. She throws her sword and clutches on to the saddle with her left hand. Captain Heneage lunges forward and buries his sword into the left breast of the rani. Grimacing with pain, the rani deflects another blow with her sword and careens into the thick of the wheeling horses. With hoarse shouts, Dost Khan and Sunder, attach themselves to her flank, and cutting maniacal arcs with their swords, they cleave a way out. The rani is now half slumped in the saddle.

Basharat Ali, Munder, and Moti Bai fall upon the British officer and almost club him to death.

Stunned by the ferocious fight and the sight of their severely injured officer, the hussars break off. The surviving Indian horsemen, numbering about twenty, ride towards the distant cloud of the rani's trail.

The British officer, bleeding severely from his head and shoulder, is exhorting his men to pursue. 'Do not let them get away . . . Rani of Jhansi,' he adds feebly as his helmeted head drops on to his chest.

For a minute, nothing happens, and then the hussars wheel around. The Indians are but distant specks of dust as they commence chase.

I can see the rani being escorted towards my humble abode, almost draped across the neck of the horse. Dost Khan and Sunder gingerly lift her from her horse and carry her into my cottage. I follow.

Dost Khan takes my hand into his own huge calloused hands and, in a hoarse whisper, says, 'Take care of her, please. She is Rani Laxmi Bai of Jhansi. May Allah bestow all his blessings upon you.' And so saying, he takes off his ruby ring and presses it into my palms.

But the rani's wrists are so slim, I think. How does she wield a sword?

At a signal from Dost Khan, Sunder removes the blood-smeared necklace of huge pearls which the rani is wearing and puts it around her neck. She gently lifts the rani's head and removes the dust-laden white pagri of the rani and winds it around her head.

With a curt nod, they jump on to their horses and ride back into the survivors, who are waiting at a considerable distance for the hussars to come closer. When the distance is less than four furlongs, the Indians charge.

Of the Indian rebels, none survive to tell the tale.

October 1858
Manikarnika Ghat, Kashi

Ever since that fateful day, I have been wandering through the jungles, lakes, fields, and dwellings to bury the secret which lies heavy on my heart.

It shall rest with me till my time comes.

December 1890
Sherghati, near Sasaram, Bihar

I am tired. My limbs are wooden, and my eyelids heavy. I must rest. Why do I look up whenever I hear the tinkle of bangles on slim wrists?

Printed in the United States
By Bookmasters